WEIRD LIES

Science Fiction, Fantasy and Strange Stories
from Liars' League

Edited by
Cherry Potts and Katy Darby

First published in UK 2013 by Arachne Press Limited
100 Grierson Road, London SE23 1NX
www.arachnepress.com
© ISBN: 978-1-909208-10-0
Edited by Cherry Potts and Katy Darby
The moral rights of the authors have been asserted
All content is copyright the respective authors.
For copyright on individual stories see page 3.
All stories originally performed at Liars' League and published
on their website 2008-2013.

Printed in the UK by TJ International, Padstow.
Many thanks to Jen at Salt Books for letting us republish *The
Last Words of Emmanuel Prettyjohn*.
Many thanks to Muireann Grealy for proof reading. Any
remaining mistakes are me not reading the proof reading
comments carefully enough. CP

CONTENTS

Introduction

Over the past eighteen months I have read around 350 stories as I delve through the Liars' League archive. Initially I was looking for themes to fit specific anthologies, and at the back of my mind was always, *there has to be a fantasy book*. I've been a passionate reader of fantasy since I was twelve.

Liars' League does bring out the weirdness in their authors, there is a certain expectation of razzmatazz when you aim at having a story read by an actor to a crowd of up to a hundred, and I think it's fair to say that a high proportion of the stories in that archive are very strange indeed.

Several fantastic stories have already been poached for the previous anthologies – notably Liam Hogan's *Rat,* Katy Darby's *Keep Calm and Carry On*; and Jason Jackson's *A Time and Place Unknown*, and sadly there were several stories we couldn't have for copyright reasons (you know who you are) which helped keep this volume a manageable size – and I am grateful to Salt for permission to reprint Jonathan Pinnock's wonderful pseudo-documentary *The Last Words of Emmanuel Prettyjohn* which appears in his collection *Dot Dash*.

We are beginning to develop a relationship with some writers with welcome returns from the Smyth brothers, James (*Let There be Light*) and Richard (*Heriot*) bringing us dystopian darkness and a psychiatric patient who might be more than he seems. David Mildon brings us *Worms' Feast*: a terrifying night in a Belgian bar; and Nichol Wilmor is completing a hat trick with his magnificently insidious *An Account of Six Poisonings*.

New to Arachne Press in the Science Fiction(ish) camp we have Peng Shepherd with *Free Cake*, in which workplace stress and enforced birthday celebrations collide with messy results. Alan Graham explores the afterlife of has-been B movie monsters in *Zwo,* Christopher Samuels takes on the Flying Dutchman in *Touchdown,* and Richard Meredith explores what we might do if we knew what was coming in *The Museum of the Future.* We meet the geek you really hope *won't* be in charge when the world looks like ending in Andrew Lloyd-Jones' *ChronoCrisis 3000* and then there is Derek Ivan Webster's desperately sad story of a lost memory in *Content Management.*

From the Fantasy wing we have Alex Smith's lazy assassin telling tales of *Icosi Bladed Scissors,* and Angela Trevithick gives an object lesson in logic in her Rapunzel retelling *Fuzzby and Coo.* Joshan Esfandiari Martin's *Daphne Changes* is another retelling, bringing myth bang up to date, and C.T. Kingston brings us a poignant tale of ice in the desert in *The Icicle,* while Ellen O'Neill slips in a gentle tale of the Unlikely Old West, with *Jethro.*

Edging into the paranormal we have the damned in Barry McKinley's *Derby of Lost Souls.* Maria Kyle's protagonist in *Candyfloss* may just be a dream, but Rebecca J Payne's *Hollow Man* is a nightmare meeting its match. Lennart Lundh's happily married couple go *Antique Shopping* with deadly results.

And then there is the hard to define - the *weird*: The vertiginously challenged young man of David Malone's *The Love Below,* Tom McKay talking to tadpoles about the meaning of life in *What Does H_2O Feel Like to the Tadpoles?,* Lee Reynoldson matching drudgery with dreams in *Haiku Short, Parakeet Prawns, Konnichiwa Peter* and David McGrath's tragic and hilarious study of the madness brought on by rejection and imprisonment in *The Elephant in the Tower.*

ChronoCrisis 3000
Andrew Lloyd-Jones

Commander Richards,

If you are reading this it means that the photonic quantum drive worked, and your journey to the future was a success. According to our telemetry data, predictions of the Earth's orbit, etc. etc., you should have appeared close to the spot where you will have hopefully found this letter.

We are all naturally dead at your point in time, as we were unable to prevent The Device from activating itself in our current timeline. However, you should, as we have discussed, be able to gather enough data in the future to enable us to work out a weakness in the Device's program in the past.

During your reconnaissance, you will need to use your digital scopes to gather visual data. We cannot be sure whether or not the pictures will continue to exist on your return, because in theory, if your mission is a success and you return with the necessary information, the future you are currently witnessing will already have ceased to exist. Although it could continue to exist, but in a different universe, in which case you will have moved through dimensions instead of time. Greg in quantum mechanics however seems to think that you move in both time *and* dimensional space as a result of your jump. He came in the other day waving a coat hanger and a globe, and this was apparently meant to demonstrate something about the space time continuum, but none of us could understand what he was on about.

Incidentally, we came up with a range of names for this mission as part of a brainstorm session we had once you'd left. Here's what we came up with:

Future Trek
Future Jump
Future Trek 3000
Future Jump 3000
Operation: Future Jump
ChronoCrisis
Time Tour
Time Trek
Time Jump
Time of Your Life
Time Trek 3000

Personally I liked ChronoCrisis, but in the end we went with Dan's suggestion which was FutureJump 3000. Basically Dan just added 3000 to everyone else's suggestions which no one else seemed to spot.

The important thing however is that now you have arrived at your destination in time, you must proceed immediately to the point on the map marked with an X. This is where you will find essential medical equipment and food supplies for your stay in the future. Our simulations predict that following the activation of The Device, and the subsequent death of all living matter on the planet, the atmosphere will have become a deadly mix of poisonous, potentially lethal gasses. That being the case, there is unlikely to be anything edible in the vicinity. It is therefore vital that you find the area marked on the map, which should be within an hour's walk or thereabouts depending on how quickly you can move, the presence of surface magma, etc.

This would be a good time to apologise for the fact that this letter and your essential medical and food supplies are not actually in the same place. While it might have made sense to put everything together, during the brainstorm Dan pointed out that if we separated everything up there was less chance of it being discovered. Also, Chloe reckoned that illogical thinking would confuse The Device, again giving us a greater chance of success.

Once you have located the medical equipment, food supplies etc. then proceed immediately to the point on the map marked by a box with a cross on it, like a church with a tower. This is the location of the hidden ECM system you'll need to mask your body's naturally occurring electrical activity from The Device's sensors. Without it you're vulnerable to detection by The Device. The point on the map marked with a circle and a cross like a church with a steeple is where we predict The Device's main defences will be located, so try not to confuse the two. The batteries to make the ECM system work are marked on the map by the symbol for a disused lighthouse.

We believe at your time in history The Device will have migrated predominantly below ground, where it will be using the earth's geothermal energy as some kind of power source, but with enough hardware above ground to allow for communication with The Device home planet. Your main target is above ground, and marked on the map with the two crossed swords. This is where Chloe's projections suggest one of The Device's main Terran interfaces will be located. We don't know exactly what this will look like, but it is vital you get close enough for detailed images of its design. Now I come to think of it, you might not have actually met Chloe. I think she started with us a couple of months after you left, having come from Cybermark Industries. She and I had a bit of an affair for a few weeks after the Christmas party, but we were both so incredibly busy, what with everything that's been going on, that it just didn't really work out. We're still good friends and stuff, which is the main thing. It's funny really, thinking about it, how none of this matters anymore, and that you're reading this after we've been dead for maybe a few thousand years.

Anyway. Make sure you don't approach The Device without the cover of the ECM or it'll detect your electrical activity and defend itself. Dan has designed the ECM to last for approximately three hours once you're in range of The Device, and after that you'll need to recharge the batteries, but you should have plenty of time. Dan started seeing Chloe not long after she and I mutually decided that it just wasn't the right time for us to get involved in a long-term relationship. I think they tried to keep it a secret from everyone but sooner or later these things come out. It was the same with her and me – let's not tell anyone, she said. It's better that way. But like I say, it's hard to keep a secret really, and I ended up seeing the two of them together outside her flat one night after they came back from dinner at a little restaurant in Tooting and the game was up. I think they're out with each other tonight, while I'm writing this in the lab. Everyone has started having Device Parties because we all know it's just a matter of time, but someone's got to make sure things get done. This letter wasn't just going to write itself. I mean, I could be out there, having a good time with some gorgeous lab assistant at some big party or whatever, but no, I'm here, with piles of data to analyse from The Device.

But that's fine. I've had this strange sense of calm come over me the past few days, and I really feel like I'm here to make a difference. After all, you're reading this, aren't you? And you're the last living creature on the planet. And where are Dan and Chloe? Atoms of dust, that's where. Forgotten debris of a miserable sham of a life. And who cares? Not me, I'll tell you that for nothing. Not you either I should think. You're probably more worried about the dangerous life-threatening mission you're on.

So anyway, you've gathered the data, taken the pictures; hopefully you've not been caught as long as Dan's crappy ECM works properly. To be honest, I wouldn't be surprised if it breaks down, he's that rubbish at his job. He spends more time on his Facebook page than he does on anything else. Just because he's got fifty thousand friends or whatever and he was voted 'Sexiest Scientist' in *Grazia*, he thinks that gives him the right to chat online with schoolgirls all day. He keeps going on about how it's important for PR and funding and that but I can't see how he's making any money out of it at all. I wouldn't mind if they sent him cash but all he gets in the post are dodgy pictures and cheap knickers.

So that's about it. The photonic batteries you'll need to get home are somewhere near the place on the map that looks like a windmill. They should work I suppose.

Good luck with 'Future Jump 3000' or whatever.

The future of the human race is in your hands.

Best regards,

Dave

Icosi Bladed Scissors
Alex Smith

'Such a hot afternoon,' Baochi said. 'Are you sure you want to die?'

Although she was a lazy assassin, Baochi had outlived the fool and the plagiarist by several centuries, insisting a daily bowl of raw beetroot borscht was the cause of her ungodly longevity (however, it must be noted that over time a good many who hankered after immortality had tried to emulate Baochi and subsist on borscht alone, but these aspirants merely suffered years of indigestion, pink-stained teeth and ruby-coloured urine, before a younger than average Death spared them from swallowing down any further bowls of borscht).

Basil, the man with aching ankles, sighed and his sigh was fat like a leopard's purr. 'I'm so tired of my ankles aching,' he said, to which Baochi replied, 'And I so weary from the heat.' She cooled herself with what appeared to be a giant fan, but closer inspection revealed the slats were blades, twenty of them, capable of simultaneous shredding; it was no fan then, rather a score of Icosi bladed scissors.

'Basil, darling, I'm in no mood for killing … I will tell you some little tale of each of my twenty blades, and then if you're still set on a gruesome demise by the Icosi-jian (*jian* is Mandarin for scissors), well, I suppose I'll have to indulge you.'

Since Baochi was superstitious about starting at the beginning, she spoke first of blade number two, that of a pair of sewing scissors, which she claimed to have plucked from the painting Degas only called his 'genre picture', although in spite of the artist's wish, commentators ever after insist the painting be named *The Rape*, and still others claim it must depict a scene from a novel by Zola.

'And this blade, aah, I *so* delight in it, Basil! From Thomas

Jefferson's scissors, the pair he used in 1819 to cut up his Bible and make it what he thought Jesus would have liked: a book without a virgin birth, a resurrection and that whole bunch of far-fetched miracles.' Baochi chortled and admired the steel damascened blade and then turned her attention to the more provincial fourth blade, one that snick-snacked in a scene from JM Coetzee's *Boyhood*.

The fifth of the blades was the most peculiar, it was a shimmering chemical splicer stolen from the history of DNA research. Thus continued Baochi until Basil and his aching ankles knew the tale of the full score.

'Now, what is your decision?' Baochi asked. 'Unchanged,' Basil replied, 'Though I have this last question: why Icosi? Why twenty blades, when one would surely suffice?'

'Why be bland,' said Baochi. 'Why be unimaginative and unremarkable? Death can be splendid.' Basil was filled with satisfaction, so unexpected and comforting, he became anxious she would change her mind.

'Do it now,' he said, 'While I'm still happy.' He closed his eyes and listened to the swish of the waves against bollards and readied himself for an end and Baochi yawned.

'Aah, surely you're too warm to die, why must it be today? I don't usually ask my clients, it makes no difference to me; I'm a professional, so you don't have to reply if you prefer not to.'

For the last time in his life, Basil sighed fat as a leopard's purr.

'It must; my bones are chock-full of cancer; and far greater is the gruesomeness my own cells have in store for me than the worst death your Icosi scissors could ever hope to achieve.'

And so with elemental grace Baochi rose and slew him.

Content Management
Derek Ivan Webster

'I'm forgetting something.' His eyes were closed; his fingertips pressed into his temples. His hands quivered as if straining to hold the skull together.

'It couldn't be that important. You never forget anything,' observed his wife as she diced peppers for a salad. The kitchen opened over a bar to the dining room table where he sat. She glanced up at intervals to regard his lone figure, elbows driving divots into the pea-green placemat.

'You look like you're praying,' she laughed.

'Just looking for something.' His fingers occasionally clinched tighter around his head, then let loose. It was a steady rhythm that resembled the draw of a pump.

'Need any help?'

He didn't respond. The mental suction continued. She went back to her salad.

He knew something was misplaced inside his head. It was a small thing but important. There were fractured references extending back to a no longer existent source. Broken lines of context fluttered at the edge of empty pockets that should have been memory. It was like trying to produce the image from a voice recording of a conversation that never took place.

'Is it someone's birthday?' he called out.

'No birthday today.' She frowned.

'This week?'

'No birthday this week.' Her frown deepened. She finished with the peppers and swept them to the side. Mushrooms would come next, but they needed retrieving from the refrigerator. She set the knife down and remained watching her husband.

He dug his thumbs deeper into the skin above his ears, leafing through the pile of internal notices that comprised his mental calendar. 'It's not Edwin's recital. That's this Saturday. Pauly has her shots a week from tomorrow. Bill-pay was yesterday. Your conference call with the board is postponed 'til next month.'

'Try something more personal,' his wife nudged.

'You know what it is?' His eyes remained closed, his face focused, but it was his turn to frown.

She shook her head. 'Are you trying to be funny?'

'I have never felt less funny.'

'And you expect me to believe you've forgotten tomorrow?'

'Tomorrow?' He opened his eyes for the first time, releasing his confusion in blinking increments. His hands stopped rubbing at his head, though the fingers remained firmly rooted. 'I've forgotten something for tomorrow? Something personal.'

'Yes.' The single word clicked into place like the sharp cock of a pistol.

'Not a birthday?'

'No.'

'A dinner? Do we have reservations?'

'Not that I'm aware.'

'Friends are coming to town?'

He was watching her now with some care. With each negation her brows were raised higher and her lips pursed tighter. The crows' feet had appeared at the corner of her eyes. That was never a good sign.

'A doctor's appointment?'

Her head shook no.

'Dancing lessons?' No. 'A night at the opera?' No. 'Tickets to Monaco?' No.

Her face had flushed full red. There was a dangerous, twitching friction beneath her chin. Her carefully applied makeup began to crack through with the tiniest of lines.

'I am so sorry, darling.' He let his hands lower slowly to the table. 'I have absolutely no idea what tomorrow is.'

'Tomorrow,' her words were so tightly drawn as to twang between syllables, 'Is our anniversary.'

They stared at each other over the open bar. Her eyes flared with a carefully checked tension. His eyes retreated into their sockets. He wet his lips. His mouth opened, started to form a thought; it was quickly abandoned.

'Well?' she demanded. 'Don't you have anything to say about our anniversary?'

'Our anniversary.' He could feel her glare cording around his throat. 'Our anniversary is tomorrow.'

She gave him one final nod: a line in the sand. One more misstep and he would no longer be able to salvage the situation. The hands clutched once again to his head. His eyes snapped closed; his mind turned in upon itself, chewing through layer after layer of insulating memory. He skittered across an endless landscape of carefully indexed data. He spun through every category, within every search parameter, across every partition. He pored over memory logs, data storage receipts, system back-up archives. He looked everywhere. He found nothing.

'Our anniversary?'

'Yes.' She strained to keep her tone level.

With no recourse left, he simply let the horrible question slip free. 'Our anniversary of what?'

His wife's face went immediately, completely, severely blank. He took a deep breath and did his best to prepare for the storm. Tempered steel came unbound behind her eyes. She would defrag him slowly until nothing of consequence remained.

The storm didn't come. Instead she breathed out a straw

house's worth of tension, wiped her hands on a dishtowel, came around the bar and took a seat at the table adjacent to his. She held out her hands and forced a smile. It was weak but he fully appreciated the attempt.

'Take my hand,' she said. He complied. 'When were we married?'

'My final go live date was –'

'When were we married?' she gently corrected him.

'On January 12th, 2020.'

'Good,' she nodded. 'And what is tomorrow's date?'

'January 12th, 2025.'

'Exactly,' she smiled. 'Now, define anniversary.'

His mind buzzed, happy to receive such a tangible activity. When he spoke his words took on a deliberate monotone: 'New Oxford, American Edition. An-ni-ver-sa-ry. Noun; the date on which an event took –'

'Next entry.'

'Special usage. The date on which a country or other institution –'

'Next entry.'

'The date on which a couple was married in a previous year. Example,' his words suddenly adopted the manufactured singsong of an overzealous actor, 'He even forgot our tenth anniversary!'

'Enough,' she said softly.

'Origin. Middle English, from the Latin anniversarius, returning yearly, from annus –'

'I said enough!' The cry brought another sharp flush to her cheeks. Her husband went silent; he showed no response. The colour soon faded and her wan smile returned.

'I want you to bookmark this entry, okay?'

He gave a small, embarrassed nod.

'Now – cross reference this to January 12th on every year of your system calendar.'

'For how long?' he asked.

'Forever.' Her smile flinched under the weight of a deep melancholy. It waited just beneath the surface and it was all she could do not to stare into its depth.

'Infinite temporality will not compute,' he warned her.

'Fine.' She flung off the shadow with a clear decision. 'Until the year twenty-one-hundred.'

His head buzzed with another sudden activity. When it was done he smiled at her. 'Until our eightieth anniversary.'

She said nothing. After a moment she squeezed his hand. 'I love you.'

'I love you, too,' he repeated.

She let his hand go. 'Search your purge folder for any files related to January 12th, Valentine's, or August 3rd.'

'Your birthday?'

'Yes,' she nodded. Another whir of focused activity.

'103 files found. Video, audio and supporting documents. Approximately 400 terabytes.'

'Good. Retrieve all files. Mark them read-only, administrative password required.'

'Did I do anything wrong, dear?'

'No. Not at all.'

He paused, considering. 'You're directing me to override my default data protocols. You installed that CMS yourself, with an intention to protect my storage capacity. Tampering with such efficiencies could prove destabilising.'

She leaned over to kiss him on the cheek. 'For this we can make an exception.'

His mind buzzed. His face showed nothing. 'If you say so, dear.'

Nodding to herself, she got up from the table and went back to the kitchen. 'The salad's almost done,' she called over the door of the refrigerator.

'Good. I'm hungry,' he heard himself saying somewhere

far above his thoughts.

His elbows went back to the table and the hands returned to the side of his head. He remembered tomorrow again. It was their anniversary. How could he have forgotten? Breathless whispers; soft skin brushing against his hardened artifice; promises of their impossible eternity: all the familiar imagery that his content management system had discarded as so much redundancy.

The sensation of something missing lingered. 400 terabytes. That was nearly a week's worth of memory documentation. In recovering the requested files his internal processor had been forced to purge an equivalent amount of data from his active archive.

His fingers continued to dig into his head. His emotion matrix continued to quiver atop an unseen vacuum.

'I'm forgetting something.' His eyes closed. He heard the clatter of dishes from the kitchen. His wife would soon have dinner ready. His mind flicked atop the inaccessible secrets locked away within his purge folder. What was in there? What was he forgetting? His mind buzzed with confusion. His hands pumped at nothing.

How important could it be?

Fuzzby & Coo
Angela Trevithick

The only window in my room is an arrow slit, which I can slip my hand through. I can see the ground through here, but my shoulder stops me slipping through and jumping to my death.

Every night I count the stars through this window. I sleep when I reach the seventy-third star, and I wake when the sun strokes my cheek. This is when my pigeon joins me. I call him Fuzzby because he has a feather that sticks up on top of his little head. He calls me Coo.

He lands on my pillow.

'Fuzzby,' I say, 'your feet are forked like the Devil's trident, but your step is light as an angel's breath.'

'Coo,' he replies.

'I'm here,' I say. I tell him this, even though we both know I'll always be here. I'm not going anywhere.

He trills a gentle song as I dance around the room, my hair trailing behind me like a wedding veil. I dream of a man in my arms, a handsome man with arms strong and eyes blue.

I dance until my stepmother comes up the stairs. She puts a key in the door, and then goes away. I know that, despite the key, the door will be locked. It's always locked. Yet still I try. I rattle the handle, and thump the wooden frame, and stamp on the floor, and yell for her to come back. Eventually I drop to the floor, drying my tears on my hair.

Fuzzby nestles into my lap until my crying stops. Then he tilts his head and says, 'Coo.'

'I'm still here,' I say, but on the word here Fuzzby flies away. He slides through the slit and before long he is a drip of ink in the distance. I cry again until my hair is too sodden to dry any more tears.

He returns the next day. I rush to him; there's something in his beak, which I take from him. He flies off again the moment the object is mine.

He's brought me a pencil. I press a finger against the tip and gasp as the sharp point pierces my flesh. I scribble on the walls. I twirl it around my fingers. I stare at it so hard that I don't hear my stepmother put the key in the lock, and I forget to scream and cry and yell.

The next morning I wake at dawn and sit by the window, waiting for Fuzzby. He arrives with a tiny square of paper in his beak. The note reads:

Prince Charming seeks Damsel in Distress. Must have fairy-tale looks and dream of a happy ending, needs g.s.o.h and to be d.t.e. Prefer n/s, s/d.

Fuzzby hops from my leg to the pencil, then rolls the pencil to me with his beak.

'But how will I send it?'

'Coo,' he says, sticking out his leg. A small blue ribbon is wrapped round his foot.

'Oh Fuzzby!' I cry. 'Oh Fuzzby you cupid, you Eros, you master of love!'

And so I begin.

Hello. I chew the end of the pencil. *A friend passed me your invitation for suitors. You seem like a dapper fellow. I should be rather –* I tap the pencil on my knee – *delighted to hear from you further. I live alone, so your correspondence will brighten my day.*

I fix the scroll to Fuzzby's leg.

'Coo,' he calls as he flies away.

The next morning he returns with a new note.

Hello mystery lady, it reads. *Your writing is light as heaven's*

clouds. *I presume you would like some information about myself.*
I enjoy fox hunting, admiring tapestries and playing cricket. I am
currently living the high life that is afforded a nobleman, but am
looking to find a new career. I was thinking perhaps social work.
Please respond promptly, as I crave to know more about you.

I reply:

To dear, kind sir. I'm afraid I have no more paper, so I must
write on the back of your letter. Your life sounds most marvellous!
Sadly, my life is dull in comparison. I do only what my confines
allow me to, as I am doomed to spend eternity in a cursed tower.
Please tell me of your life of freedom, as it helps me to feel like I
am living.

I send Fuzzby away, but he doesn't return the next day. He doesn't return the day after that either. I don't sleep, I don't eat, I don't dance, I don't cry. I just wait.

Weeks pass. I make an effort to sleep, but the slightest sound wakes me. Soon I feel that I can't lift my arms to brush my hair, or my lungs to let in oxygen.

Then one night, just as sleep finally fills my veins, I hear a fluttering.

'Coo.'

There he is, sitting on the windowsill!

'Coo,' Fuzzby says again. I lunge across the room, but just as I reach him he leaves once again. I peer out the window, and can see Fuzzby on the ground, walking in circles around a dirty, scratched man. His clothes are ragged and his feet are bare.

'Is it you?' I call.

'It is I,' he responds. 'I have come to rescue my damsel in distress.'

'Thank you,' I say, 'but there is no way.'

'I'll climb to your window.'

'I have nothing for you to climb.'

'Your bed sheets.'

'I have only the one. Even if I tore it, it wouldn't be long enough. Besides, it would not be strong enough to hold you.'

So the man begins to cry. He says,

'I have walked so far, I have searched for so long. Finally your pigeon brought me to you. Surely there must be a way!'

I join his crying. I reach for my hair to dry my tears, and as I hold it I realise that it has grown considerably. It's thick as rope, and surely as long. Gathering my hair up, I feed it out of the window.

'What are you doing?' he calls.

'Take the end!'

I stand with my back to the window, bracing myself against the wall. His hands grip my hair. He is heavier than I expected, but I bite my tongue against the pain. As he climbs, his huffs of breath get nearer and nearer. Then suddenly the pressure on my hair loosens. He has an arm through the window! I try to move away, but my hair is partially trapped under him.

'Don't move!' he says. 'I'll fall if you move!'

I stand very still, my back to him, my hair pinned between his body and the tower wall.

'This window's too small!' he says. 'I won't fit through!'

'Oh,' I say. 'Of course you won't. We really should have thought of that before.'

So we stay, me terrified of moving an inch, and him gripping the wall through the window. Bit by bit, his arm slips. I cry tears I can't dry. They fall free down my cheeks as we both wait for the end.

Derby of Lost Souls
Barry McKinley

We were fifteen years old and we didn't have enough grey matter between us to form one small but sensible idea. We were dumber than the day was long, and this was high summer, 1975. Standing at the edge of the field, we did our best to conceal the lingering stupidity in a blue haze of cigarette smoke. We didn't want Tom Kavanagh to look into our eyes and see the accumulated nothing.

'Opium is just like turnips or spuds,' he said in his Bogman accent. 'You weed it, you water it and you walk away from it. There isn't going to be any funny business, because funny business would land the pair of you in reform school…'

Eight acres of bursting poppies leaned one way and then the other under a blue Irish sky.

'We'll drop the hut down before lunch, so you have some place to get out of the sun, but don't be spending all day inside, or it'll be taken away just as quickly. Am I making myself clear?'

We nodded our vacant heads.

Tom turned and left the field. He could have opened the five-barred gate but he chose instead to vault the wire. It might have been a cool move for a younger man, but he snagged the tip of his boot and fell on his face, and then refused to look back because he knew we were sniggering. He got into the old Bedford and drove away, humiliated.

'What a moron,' said Paul. 'I can't believe I'm putting up with this crap for twelve quid a week.'

'Twelve quid,' I echoed, and then we both laughed and

laughed until it wasn't funny anymore. Paul spat on his hands as if he were about to do some serious work, but then he just leaned on his hoe and looked off towards the hills.

'Pink Floyd play Knebworth in July,' he said, telling me a piece of information that everybody in the entire galaxy was fully aware of. It felt like he was just trying to rub it in because we would unquestionably be stuck here, in this arse of a town, excluded from the party.

'Shine on you crazy diamond,' he said, quoting the Floyd.

'Wish you were here,' I replied.

'Wish I wasn't.'

We looked at the flowers waving in the field and said nothing for quite a while. It was nice. It wasn't a strain. We didn't have to think.

A little after twelve o'clock, a flatbed lorry pulled up with our hut on the back: an eight by eight box made from ship-lapped pine; it smelled of creosote and pipe smoke. The lorry driver and his helper winched it down onto the tarmac and we had to drag it into the field. I left the door open hoping that it would air out, but the ingrained smell refused to depart.

Paul dodged inside, then looked out the window and snarled, 'Get off my land'. He pointed the handle of a rake at me and made a 'Kaboom' noise. I dropped to the ground, clutching my chest. I lay there, looking at the cloudless sky, wondering why I wasn't spinning off the planet, into the blueness above.

'Do you believe in gravity?' I asked.

Paul came into my frame of vision and looked down.

'Do you know anything about this stuff?' he said, nodding towards the poppies.

'Only what I read in the National Geographic.'

'Do we need any special tools?'

'Just a sharp blade,' I said.

He pulled out a Stanley knife and waved it around.

'Would you sell your soul to see the Floyd in concert?'

'Sure,' I said.

Paul made a slashing gesture across his palm with the Stanley knife and before I could get out of the way, two or three droplets of bright red blood came splashing down on my cheek.

'Hey! What are you doing?' I said, jumping up.

'Let's sign our satanic pact in blood.'

'I don't want your blood all over me.'

He took a paper tissue out of his pocket and held it tight in his fist. I took the knife and nicked the back of my middle finger.

'Our souls for Pink Floyd and Knebworth,' we chanted as we mixed our blood together.

Then, the Angelus bells in town started ringing.

'Wooooohhh!' said Paul, in a ghostly warble. 'That's the devil clanking his balls together.'

'When does he come to pick up our souls?'

'I don't know,' said Paul, lighting a match and flicking it into the air, 'I think maybe when you're in your fifties.'

At lunchtime, a stream of cars headed into town. The men and women from the offices in the Research Institute looked lost and meaningless as they gripped their steering wheels. Tom Kavanagh cruised past slowly, craning his neck, watching us as we weeded on the headland with fake energy. He beeped the horn twice but we didn't look up.

'What a moron,' said Paul.

After the last car departed, we got down to business. We slid into the middle of the field, taking care not to leave any obvious path through the poppies. Paul slashed away with the blade and I followed close behind, squeezing the milky juice from the bulbs. After forty-five minutes, we went back to the hut, ate our sandwiches and drank our tea. We did this every day for the next two weeks, ending up with a quantity of gum about the size of a tennis ball. We wrapped it in a supermarket bag and hid it under a cool cluster of dock leaves at the end of the field.

Paul was the one who came up with the idea of selling the tennis ball to Wuzzy Ryan. Wuzzy was a red-haired boy with powerless eyes. He came from a grim home where nothing ever worked out. There was an older brother called Scuzzy and a younger sister called Huzzy. Scuzzy had been in the army for less than two months; he was kicked out when they discovered he had a tendency to hurt people when they were asleep. Huzzy was a scary combination of shapeliness and mental retardation. Whenever she answered the dog-scratched door to their council home, she would turn sideways, making you squeeze past her speed bumps. She licked her lips and batted her eyelids, a lot. It was as if a space alien had hijacked a human body, but never learned to work it properly – Paul once summed up the entire family by saying that somebody had broken into their gene shed and robbed a bunch of chromosomes.

Wuzzy was alone in the house when we called. He had just painted his bedroom walls with one thin coat of 'midnight sky' emulsion and blotches of the previous colour came through, like pasty skin under a black nylon stocking. We sat on the bed. Wuzzy weighed the tennis ball in his hand, and then offered us twenty tabs of acid, but we said no; what we wanted mostly was cash.

'How much?'

'Fifty quid for the lot.'

Wuzzy batted his eyes and licked his lips. In the semi-darkness of the room, he looked just like his crazy sister, but without the speed bumps.

'I might give you thirty,' he said.

'Thirty-five,' said Paul, 'Along with six tabs of acid.'

Wuzzy nodded and then picked out a small sheet of

blotting paper from the middle of a Sven Hassel book. We were on our way to Knebworth.

*

Recently I've been getting the feeling that somebody is standing behind me. It's not a nice feeling and it doesn't matter how much I drink or smoke or bang-up, it never goes away. It's like something permanent and dark is hovering right back there, just behind my head. I think I know what it is, but I'm afraid to say.

Last week I ran into Paul. He was coming out of the bookie shop on Kelly's Corner and he was counting money.

'Did you win?' I asked.

'Nah! Just counting what I didn't lose.'

I haven't seen much of Paul over the years. A long time ago he turned into a bald, fat guy and it looks like he's going to stay that way. The Knebworth weekend was probably the last time we were close and neither of us remembers much about it. Before we got on the ferry to England, we dropped the acid and smoked the small blob of opium we had managed to keep. Somewhere outside Chester, everything started to blur. I vaguely remember running down a street shouting, 'Thank you Satan,' with Paul charging along beside me going, 'You're a top man Satan, top man.'

I asked Paul if any strange stuff had happened to him recently, but he couldn't think of anything. In fact, he said, he'd probably welcome something peculiar because it would break up the endless boredom in this arse of a town. He asked me if I was working and I told him the truth: people who hire people don't hire people like me.

We should have turned to walk in opposite directions, but I had a question I needed to ask.

'Do you ever think about your soul?'

He thought it was a joke and he turned up the sole of his

shoe for a moment and studied it.

'I'm worried about damnation,' I said.

He asked me if I needed some money but I said no; nevertheless, he squeezed a fiver into my hand and I didn't give it back.

'I think the devil is behind me,' I said.

Paul looked embarrassed. He wanted to turn and walk away but he was probably worried I would follow, talking loudly about supernatural stuff.

'Don't you remember the weekend we went to Knebworth?' I asked.

'Long time ago,' he said, looking into my eyes, trying to peel back thirty-five layers on the onion.

'Long time ago,' I repeated.

The speed of the town slowed down all around us. Moving traffic looked like it was parked. Birds stopped flying in mid-air. And I could hear things. I could hear Paul's heart beating, the blood running around in his veins, the thoughts jumping across the tiny spaces inside his head. I listened to those thoughts, but there was nothing connected to the field, the hut, the Stanley knife, the blood and the bargain with Lucifer, and then I realized.

'You're already taken,' I said.

He looked genuinely puzzled, but I knew he was an empty canister, a spiritual void, a soulless creature forced to walk around this dreary place, eating and drinking and smoking and backing horses. I could see no pleasure inside those eyes.

'The devil has already snatched your soul,' I said.

Paul put his hand on my shoulder and stepped around me. With the spell broken, the whole town started moving again. The sound of a horse race, all numbers and enthusiasm, came belting from the TV in the bookie shop.

'Shine on you crazy diamond!' I shouted after him.

'Wish you were here!' he shouted back.

'Wish I wasn't,' I replied.

I looked in through the open door and watched the action on a big flat screen as it switched from Chepstow to Newmarket. The favourite in the 4:25 was a horse called Mephistofilly, and I wondered if she too was a sign. I placed a bet with the five euros I got from Paul; it was a long shot at fifty-to-one but I knew I had to take it. Supposing the devil was offering me the opportunity to win back my soul. Supposing I won. I took a seat in the corner of the shop, closed my eyes, and waited for the race to start.

The Icicle
C.T. Kingston

Once upon a time, in a far-away desert kingdom, there lived a prince, the darling of his people: strong and tall, with skin golden as the shifting sands, and eyes black as the desert night. On his twenty-first birthday a magnificent feast was arranged, and chieftains and merchants and artists came many miles to honour their young lord.

The occasion was magnificent and the guests giddy with wonders, but as the prince entered the dining hall he gasped. A beautiful woman stood before him, quite naked, quite still. She was the loveliest thing he had ever seen, and the strangest; for her smooth, slender body was glistening and transparent, as though made of the clearest glass.

'What is she?' he wondered aloud.

'A sculpture in ice for your pleasure, my lord,' said a deep, foreign voice. The prince turned, and saw a muscular, light-haired man, dressed in rough furs despite the desert heat.

'Ice?' said the prince. 'What is that?'

'Allow me to explain, sir. My land is so far North that in winter, water freezes, becoming solid as stone, so a man may carve figures out of it.'

'Extraordinary,' murmured the prince, glancing again at the white, shining woman.

'She is truly my masterpiece,' sighed the Northern sculptor. 'A shame she will not last.'

'What! What do you mean?'

'Ice must thaw, my lord, and return to the water it once was. See, at her heart, there is a tiny flaw? It is the icicle from which she was formed. Water ran over it, and froze, creating a great crystal, and from that I carved her. She will have melted away by tomorrow.'

The prince touched his finger to the ice-maiden's face; it came away bearing a cold drop of water, like a single tear.

'What a pity,' he said softly.

The prince ate and drank, but tasted nothing; not the peacock's eggs nor the spiced sea-flowers, nor the lion's-tongue soup, and the heady wines had no effect on him. He longed only for the feast to finish so he could be alone with the beautiful statue, to admire her in solitude. So life-like was she, that several times during the banquet he glanced at her and started, for the way the candle-light played upon her gleaming body, he almost thought that she moved and breathed.

At last the revellers rose and left to begin the dancing. When the doors had closed behind them, the prince breathed a trembling sigh, and stepped towards the ice-maiden, his arms outstretched. His hands prickled as he clasped them about her narrow waist. He ran his fingers along the smooth curve of her arms and down the frosted waves of her long, silver hair.

'What a shame you are not a real woman,' he whispered aloud, 'for I should make you mine.'

And he kissed the shimmering hardness of her frozen lips, tasting ice-water on his tongue. Withdrawing, he gazed at her one last time, then turned away.

'Do not go,' said a soft voice, like the chiming of tiny crystals.

The prince whipped around in astonishment. The ice-maiden stood motionless. But then her frozen eyelids opened and she blinked, once, and stared at him with eyes blue as glaciers. Her cold lips parted, revealing crystalline teeth, and she spoke again.

'Do not leave me, now you have awoken me!'

'What witchery is this?' gasped the prince, amazed and a little afraid.

'No witchery,' said the ice-maiden, 'only what you wished for. Your kiss has given me life, and I am yours.'

*

Beneath the palace lay the wine-cellars, an echoing complex of caves which were always cool and still, even in the height of summer, and it was there, to a secret chamber of which only he had the key, that the prince took the ice-maiden. There he kept her to preserve her frozen beauty; there he visited her to feel the cold delight of her limbs against his, and taste the icy meltwater of her mouth. Her accommodation was simple and bare, for women of ice need neither food nor fire to live; love alone is enough for them – and so the ice-maiden believed herself quite happy.

One night, the prince entered her chamber dressed in satin and cloth-of-gold, seeming strange and offhand.

'My love, what is the matter?' she asked. 'Have you something on your mind?'

He smiled distractedly. 'My father died yesterday, so I was crowned today, and must send for my bride tomorrow.'

'Your bride?' she said, in a voice as soft as settling snow.

'Yes, my fiancée, the princess of the Plains,' he said. 'We have been betrothed since we were born. Have I not spoken of her before? She visits often: you must have seen her.'

'I have been down here since I awoke,' said the ice-maiden quietly. 'I see nobody but you.' And her eyes in the candlelight sparkled like wet diamonds.

'Of course,' said the prince hastily. 'I forgot. Well, the wedding will be very magnificent, I'm sure, but rather a bore. You wouldn't want to see it anyway.'

'I should like to see her,' she said.

'Why?' asked the prince, warily.

'Because she must be very beautiful to take you from me.'

He laughed. 'Oh, this is politics merely: the union of two great kingdoms! She is lovely, to be sure, and indeed I love her, for I have known her since childhood, but it is a matter of duty too.' He leaned forward and took her cold hands in his warm ones. 'Besides, she won't take me from you! I shall visit you as often as ever, and everything will be just as it was.'

'So I am to be your … mistress?' she said, and the icicle of her heart cracked a little.

The prince looked puzzled. 'Why, what else could you be? You are exquisite, certainly, but you are a woman of ice. I need a real, live wife, warm and fruitful, to give me heirs. You can never do that.'

She cupped her frozen palms about his face. The prince shivered.

'Who knows what could happen? The kiss of desire made me live: could not the kiss of true love make me a true woman, such as you could marry?'

Her snow-white lips parted, and a question trembled in her ice-blue eyes.

'It cannot be,' said the prince, in a harsh voice that brooked no argument. 'Besides, it is all arranged. Do not grieve, my dear. She shall be my queen of flesh and blood above, and you shall be my ice-queen below.'

And he stood, and brushed the pale frost of her tears from his velvet cloak, and left her alone in the darkness.

*

And so it was: for what choice had the ice-maiden, if the prince would not give her life by giving her love? She must stay as she was, a living soul in a body of ice, hiding away in a cold underground chamber from the fatal heat above, burning with pain and melting a little every time her lover embraced her.

At night, now, after he was gone, tears dropped from her

eyes like glittering hail, and though she tried to gather them up, they scattered and melted. She was weeping herself away, and she felt herself shrinking, just as a sliver of ice held in the mouth will eventually melt to nothing.

Almost a year passed, and one day the prince arrived, clad this time not in velvets and satins, but in chainmail and armour, and wearing an expression of terrible solemnity.

The ice-maiden started up in alarm. 'Where are you going, dressed for battle? Oh, do not leave me! I could not bear it!'

He touched her face gently with a mailed fist.

'I must go, my dear. The Western chieftains are becoming restless, and their rebellion needs crushing. I will not lose all that my father gained.'

He held out the key of her chamber.

'Here,' he said. 'Lock the door behind me, and let no-one but me in, however loud they knock. I shall return.'

And he lifted his visor, and pressed his warm, living mouth to her frozen one, his lips burning hers.

*

For a month the ice-maiden stayed in her cavern, tortured by dreams of the prince dying on the battlefield, weeping blood from many wounds. She wondered how his queen was bearing his absence, and thought fiercely that if she had been a flesh-and-blood woman, she should have insisted on accompanying her husband, even to the field of death.

She tried not to think too often of the queen, for it made the icicle of her heart shiver and crack, but what else had she to do, alone and friendless? She wished sometimes that her rival would die in some terrible accident, and the prince return to find his wife dead. Then, she thought, he would come to her and kiss her on the mouth with the kiss of true love, and she would feel life burn like a fever in her icy veins, and would become his queen of flesh-and-blood at last.

One night she heard the cellarmen outside her door for the first time ever.

'The doctor asked for the strongest stimulants we have,' said one, 'This is where we keep the Southern Tiger-Spirit.'

'D'you think she'll live?' asked another, rougher and deeper.

'If this stuff doesn't save the queen,' said the first voice adamantly, 'nothing can.'

And their footsteps echoed away.

The ice-maiden's eyes widened in the darkness. So her dreadful, secret wish had come true! Her rival was gravely ill, her life despaired of! She felt guilty and elated, and could not sleep for thinking of the sick woman, lying in bed helpless, perhaps gazing her last upon the world. She yearned to look at last into the eyes of her rival and see who it was her prince had loved since childhood; had loved beyond even her.

She unlocked the heavy door of her chamber. All was silent as she crept up to the palace above. The midnight corridors were cool, and so the ice-maiden melted only a little as she emerged into a world of pink-and-gold marble, silver mirrors and gauze curtains stirring like ghosts in the night breeze. She followed the sounds of lamentation to the chamber where the sick woman lay, watching from the shadows behind a pillar, still as the statue she had once been.

A white-bearded man emerged, shaking his head sadly.

'The fire-spirit has had no effect,' he said. 'All we can do now is let nature take its course. If her fever does not break tonight, she will be dead by morning.'

At this, the assembled servants set up such a weeping and caterwauling that the doctor scolded them for disturbing their mistress, chasing the whole mourning crowd away from her door.

The ice-maiden, quiet and motionless in her dark corner, wondered at the affectionate devotion shown by the servants.

She had always imagined her rival as an imperious, regal figure, distant and remote, a little like the prince in his black moods. Perhaps the queen was not so forbidding and magnificent as she had dreamed? No matter: her curiosity would be satisfied soon.

Softly, with no more sound than water dropping onto stone, she crossed the hall and slipped through the door.

The queen's chamber was fearfully hot and stuffy; windows had been opened, but the sultry midsummer air and the heat from the feverish body in the bed made the ice-maiden recoil. She conquered her fear, however, and approached to gaze upon the sleeping face of the woman her prince loved.

She must have been beautiful once, but her loveliness had been ravaged by the consuming sickness. Her young cheeks, once, perhaps, soft and plump, were sunken and hectic, flushed fiery-red by the blazing fever. Her pale gold hair was dark with wild sweat, and her hands, bone-thin and wasted, clutched deliriously at the silken bedclothes.

'Why,' thought the ice-maiden, 'she's only a girl!' And cold pity shivered the icicle at her heart. She stroked the queen's brow, and as the icy fingers touched her skin, the girl's green eyes flew open, staring sightless and wild. The woman of ice leaned over to look into those eyes, and as she did so, a drop of ice-water fell from her cheek and landed on the mouth of the dying girl.

'Ah!' mumbled the queen, licking her cracked lips avidly, and 'Oh, it's so refreshing! Please doctor, more water!'

The ice-maiden shrank back. The heat rose from the queen's body in fierce waves; she was burning up like paper.

'Doctor,' whispered the queen, in a voice as dry as the desert sands, 'do not let me die before I see my husband again. That is all I ask. And oh, just a drop more of that sweet cold water.'

The ice-maiden stared at the thin child in the bed, the green eyes roving the shadows of the bedchamber, wide and blind. She cannot even see me, she thought in wonder. Perhaps I am not real after all, for only the prince saw me move; only his touch made me live.

She thought of the prince fighting on a Western hillside; of him returning, wounded and triumphant, to find his bride dead. She thought of the tears that would rain from his night-black eyes, down his golden cheeks, and she was surprised to find that there were tears running freely down her own frozen face; not icy, hard little hailstones, but real tears, warm and sweet. She was melting in the heat of the sick-room; she must leave the dying queen for her cold cellar chamber at once, or die herself. But she could not. For the prince loved the queen, and her death would kill him as surely as a spear or axe.

And the ice-maiden realised that it did not matter that her heart was of ice; for it could break and melt like any heart of flesh-and-blood. And nor did it matter whether or not the prince loved her, or had ever loved her; only that she had loved him.

She put her hand on the queen's hot brow, though it scorched her to touch, and heard her sigh. Then she laid a finger across the pale, feverish lips, and watched her frozen flesh melt into the dying girl's parched, thirsty mouth.

*

When the doctor entered the chamber the next morning he wondered if, perhaps, there had been a rain-storm in the night, for he was astonished to find the queen alive and sleeping peacefully, her cheeks pale and her brow cool, in a bed which was entirely drenched with icy water.

'Some miracle has wrought this!' he thought, and, gazing closer, he saw with a peculiar start of curiosity that between her parted lips lay an icicle, slender as a chip of diamond, which, even as he stared at it, melted away.

Let There Be Light
James Smyth

The world stopped turning a long time ago, and no-one knows why. Whatever force, or impetus, that drives us suddenly disappeared. Whatever cosmic hand that spins the planet withdrew. It's difficult to understand. There's plenty about it in the ancient books, of course, but nobody reads those any more. Nobody reads much of anything anymore. We barely have enough fuel to light the hospitals and the council chambers – there's not enough to go around. We have one lamp in the house, and we only light it for one hour a day, at dinner time. There's no light for reading. There's no light for anything.

I wonder if it has to be this way. It seems as though we've forgotten so much. Across the land lie factories, hulking and abandoned, with their unknowable machinery sitting there in the dark, unused. Every now and again the councils launch some kind of project, or initiative, in an attempt to get them running again, but they always run out of steam before too long. No-one has any enthusiasm for it. It's something to do with the darkness – the lack of light and the lack of hope. I am twenty three years old and I have never seen a sunrise. Our people don't understand the concept of a new dawn.

Sometimes I dream about the sun. I dream of lying in an enormous field, so big I can't see where it ends. It is light, impossibly light, and it is warm. Not like the warmth of the fire, which dwindles as soon as you step away from it, but a warmth that fills the air, and as I stretch my arms and legs I can feel it, pressing gently on my bare skin. It is so bright I have to close my eyes, and still I can see the red on the inside of my eyelids. Nothing else happens in the dream, and that's fine. It's enough just to lie there in that summer paradise. And then I wake, beneath my rough, heavy covers, and feel the cold on my face, and my heart is heavy with a sense of loss.

I must travel east. People are always talking about it, but no-one ever does. It's a long way to go. There are vehicles everywhere, strange and alien vessels with wheels and wings and rusting fuel tanks, but nobody knows how to make them work. Nobody can remember the last time they moved anywhere. So I must walk, and if what little geography I have learned is correct, then there are thousands of miles to cover. But I don't care if it takes me the rest of my life. To see that glimpse of light in the sky – not like the stars, which hang limp and drab in the firmament – but a light that stays, and grows, and spreads as you walk towards it. To see the sun – the very words seem impossible – that would be the most perfect thing of all. That would be worth a lifetime.

And yet, even as I say these words, I know the truth. Such a voyage cannot be made. I have no light, and there are seas and mountains and deserts to cross. I have a compass, a very old compass, that was left to me by my grandfather, but it won't be enough, even if I can read it by the starlight. I would have to build a boat, and I don't know how. I would have to catch my own food. The animals are not so plentiful these days as they were in the olden times, and so many of them are underground. It is such a long way in the dark.

There is a girl I know. I say 'know'. I mean 'love'. There is a girl I love. She is eighteen years old and she lives in a house down the road. She is an orphan and she stays with her grandmother. And though she is young, there is something about her, something in the way she speaks, that makes her seem old. She seems very old. Older than the oldest person I know. Her voice is low and soft, like the wind, and though I have never seen her face in the light, I know she is beautiful.

Some evenings we sit on her porch, swaddled in blankets, and she lets me lay my head on her lap. She puts her warm hand on my forehead, and she talks to me. She tells me that she remembers what it was like before, when the world turned, and the sun rose, and everything was all right.

'Do you mean you dream about it,' I say, 'Because sometimes I –'

'No.' She cuts me off. 'I remember it.'

I know this can't be true. Nobody remembers those days. Nobody is old enough. And yet, when she strokes my hair, and speaks to me in that voice, I can almost believe it.

'Tell me about it,' I say.

And she talks, for hours, about the world as it was, the world as it still is, on the other side of the planet. She talks of huge cities, of towering glass buildings that reflect the sun and flash like beacons. About cars and aeroplanes – not the rusting hulks that litter our landscape – but brightly coloured machines that stream through the sky and zip down the long black roads that flow endlessly out into the countryside. She talks of parks and fields and enormous trees that crane their branches towards the light, and of birds – tiny, winged creatures that swoop and glide through the air. There are no birds here anymore. Everything lives underground, where it is warm.

She points up at the sky, and tells me that the stars, those hateful, sickly stars, are all suns. Each one is a sun like our own, only many millions of miles away. I don't know how she knows this. She tells me that one day we may be able to travel there, in vast ships, and find a new world, a world that spins. I imagine being there with her, sitting on a porch like this, and watching our first star rise, but I don't tell her this. I don't want her to laugh at me. I don't want her to know that I love her.

'Tell me about the path,' I say.

She says that there is a path, that starts not so very far from here. It leads to the East. It was built very long ago, by our ancestors, the ones who could still remember the sun. Before we started to forget everything. The path is long, and winds through the mountains and the deserts, but it is lit, with lamps that never burn out. Once you reach a lamp, you have to squint your eyes, and right out in the distance you will be able to see the next one. So you follow the lamps, and after many years you reach the other side of the world.

'Just imagine,' she says, 'Seeing that light for the first time. Just a faint glimmer on the horizon to begin with. Days of walking, and still only the faintest hint of sun. But then, after weeks, after months, the glimmer grows, and starts to fill the sky. It gets warm. We take off our hats and our overcoats, because we don't need them any more. The sky is blue. Just imagine that! A blue sky, from east to west.'

I just listen, as she talks on. I know that soon she will ask me to come with her, to find the path. It's what she always asks. Only ten miles outside the village, she says. Usually I nod and murmur general agreement, but I know that ten miles is a long way. I have never been more than a few hundred feet outside the village. There is danger out there in the darkness.

Tonight is different, though. I feel as though something inside me has suddenly awoken. I feel like a light has come on. I sit here, on my bed, waiting for a knock on the window. I have packed a bag. She will be here within the hour, and together we will set off, in search of daylight. I don't know what we will eat. I don't know what we will do for shelter, out there in the wilderness. And I know, deep down, that there is no path. There are no magical lamps. We are going to our deaths, and we will die one night, in the cold and the black, huddled together and dreaming an impossible dream. We will never see the sun.

It's something to do with the darkness – the lack of light

and the lack of hope.

I twitch back the curtain and stare into the sky. The stars are there, as always. They are the nearest I will ever get to sunlight. A million, million miles.

I see her coming across the field, her white dress just visible in the night. I want to draw her into my room, and to hold her, and make her forget this whole thing. To keep her safe. To keep us both safe. But I know I won't. I will follow her, like the sunflowers in her stories follow the sun. She is the brightest thing in the sky, and all I know is that I want to be near her.

I open the window and hold out my hand, and she takes it with both of hers.

'Are you ready?' she says, in that low, soft voice.

And I'm not, I'm really not. But I lever myself up on to the window ledge, and I swing my legs over. The ground is cold and hard and the air is freezing. It clasps itself around me. I look at her, and she moves her face close to mine.

'Don't worry,' she says. 'We're going to make it.'

I can see her eyes in the starlight. I wonder what I would give to see them in the daylight. Away from the two or three scattered lights in the village, the world looks a dark and awful place.

'I know,' I say, and together we begin to walk.

The Love Below
David Malone

My brother suffers from Kunderan vertigo; a heady, insuperable desire to fall upward. There is very little we can do other than try to weigh him down. On the day of his baptism, the priest informed my parents that David had a 'heavenly calling'. He meant it literally.

His condition dictates that he varies in lightness. Upon leaving the house my mother, who is more of a worrier than my father, stuffs books into his coat pockets. She does this to quell her fear that one day his feet will simply up and abandon the pavement.

'We have to take precautions, Alma,' I am reminded as she wedges hardbacks into his duffel.

When he told us he was travelling to America, my mother laughed until she cried.

'Alone?'

A nod.

'For the whole summer?'

Another nod.

She brushed it off as a New Year's whim, but a ticket arrived in spring and by late May he'd bought a backpack. On the first of June they drove him to the airport and checked him in. She told him he didn't have to go, that she hadn't meant to laugh across the turkey, and if that's what all of this was about – proving that he could – then she was sorry. My father simply hugged him and told him to remember to think. Before he left them for the departure gate she ran into the airport bookshop, purchased *The Almanac of Great American Landmarks* – the heaviest thing she could find – and heaved it into his hand luggage.

Two weeks later we received a postcard; a Black Bear with a red greeting printed above it that read: *Hello from the Catskill Mountains, New York State*. The reverse told us he'd landed a job at Timber Lake Camp teaching swimming lessons to rich Jewish kids. My mother's mind veered from pole to pole.

'New York? How will he ever keep his footing in New York? Even the buildings there refuse to touch!'

And with a flip of her axis:

'He's up in the mountains, I mean real American mountains. You *do* remember what he was like in Scotland that time? He's halfway up already!'

My father brought her back down to earth with his own brand of logic.

'He's with Jewish kids, love – those kids are real thinkers, nobody does angst like the Jews. He'll be swamped in it all, heavy as a lead balloon.'

'Do you really think so?' she smiled.

It seemed to do the trick.

By the time I received his letter, he was already on the road. It told me that camp was fun, the people kind and the campers surprisingly upbeat. He'd been promoted to Head Swim Instructor by the Camp Director and was fast becoming *persona grata* for all tips on swim techniques – except diving – which, given his buoyancy, didn't surprise me. A half-page account introduced me to one of his pupils, a little black girl called Nabilla who wasn't a Jew but in fact the chef's daughter: her camp fees waived as part of his contract. A poor swimmer, she moved through the water with a heavy, slothish crawl that he found inspiring:

If only you could see how dense she is, Alma, all that grace in her resistance.

He left for New York City with Kailer, a Canadian from Edmonton. In his native town Kailer had lifeguarded at a pool inside what was then the world's largest mall. Fired for occupational neglect, which in reality meant leaving two women to fight it out while he finished the closing pages of *The Minotaur Takes a Cigarette Break*, Kailer had headed for the States.

'Screw that, Dave.' he told my brother on the first day of camp. 'No way was I letting some ring-nosed super-dykes steal my money-shot.'

At camp, Kailer had discovered the Almanac David anchored across his chest at night, replaced it with the two copies of *Oranges Are Not the Only Fruit* that Eisenberg and Molasky seemed to cradle and, leafing through the glossy images, mistook what he saw for a quietly-burning dream. By morning he'd decided a Great American Road Trip, 'Coast to Corn-Fed Coast' would be the perfect antidote to eight weeks of TLC. He gave himself a week in the city to rustle together a band of strays game for the ride – the obligatory $100 in-hand for the purchase of a van – while my brother was left to drift along wide Manhattan avenues punctuated by stores, galleries and gallery-stores. By the fifth night in the hostel David was complaining of light-headedness.

'Don't worry buddy, we're leaving this dump real soon,' his friend assured him, beating abandoned *Lonely Planet* guides into his cargo shorts. 'You can hold out, right? We're so close Dave; one more roadie is all we need …'

He spent their final day perched on grass tips in Central Park, watching clouds rise. A metallic *He-llo* rang several times through his ears before he registered the word. The girl at his side fumbled with a small plastic device and nudged it toward him; the flashing cursor on the screen asked him to *Please Type*. His own *hello* spewed out as a garbled, incomprehensible noise. It delighted her no end. Voicelessly she answered his questions:

Ko-rean.
Se-oul.

Skye.

Father's cre-dit card.

Everything.

The grass collapsed beneath him when she invited herself on the trip.

The route they agreed on was little more than a shallow scribble on a fold-out map, dipping down from New York through Alabama, Mississippi and Texas, skimming into Mexico and back up through the desert states into California. By the time they reached Lake Powell they had lost a Corsican Francophobe to Baton Rouge and a Pole to Chihuahua.

'The second largest man-made lake in the States, Dave!' Kailer pointed out from the pages, beer in hand, as they baked on a cliff-edge.

'*Jump?*' Skye asked him.

Intonation was a difficult thing to gauge, but the charcoal smudges she called eyes told him she was serious.

'*Hea-vy,*' she reassured him, grabbing his hand.

She fell like a brick tied to a balloon, hitting the water with a vaporous slosh. When they surfaced she was all bubbles and light, whooping a high-pitched shriek he decided was joy. She squeezed him tightly as he kicked them back to land.

When he reached the top he wanted to do it again, wanted to fall and crash into the blue; wanted it all to hit him like a cold, wet punch to the face. He couldn't find her translator, so gestured his desire to her with an arc of the hand instead. She shook her head at him as she dried herself in slow strokes. Giddy with thought, he snatched the Almanac from his dozing friend's face, skipped toward the edge and turned to her. She shouted excited words he didn't understand but smiled at, hugging the weight to his chest as he jumped up and down. Her Korean took on a tone of urgency he only grasped after he felt the hollow crunch and jab into the roof of his foot that sent him backwards. Her little voice flew out with him and into the void. Before she slipped from his sight he memorised her mouth, her expression; that undeniable flag of disappointment draped across her face as the lip of ledge severed him from her. He was home two days later.

My mother took it as a personal validation that he had cut his trip short. Such was her delight at seeing him that she dismissed the fact he was becoming transparent, his hair so wispy-light it was barely there.

'I'm glad the American Dream didn't swallow you up,' she told him between kisses of his brow.

He didn't speak for the first two days, which we put down to jet-lag – until he explained to me with a pen that he couldn't, that he'd somehow lost his voice, misplaced it somewhere. I screamed when I walked into his room and found him collapsed on the ceiling.

They took him to all of the doctors they could find; anatomists, psychologists, structural behaviourists; but each reserved the same blank response. It was my father's suggestion in the end that saved us:

'We'll line his room with lead. Nothing can move through lead.'

So that's where he's been for the last four weeks, with a television that no longer has reception and a bookcase bereft of his favourite author.

'No Kundera under any circumstances!' we're now reminded each morning before she leaves for work.

I ask her why we're doing this, if it's even the right thing to do, if weight is necessarily better than lightness, down better than up, if there's even a distinction between the two. She only understands the first.

'It's because we love him,' she tells me as she closes the door.

It's the heaviest truth I know.

Haiku Short, Parakeet Prawns, Konnichiwa Peter
Lee Reynoldson

I often dream that I am Japanese.

My mornings are cold, dark, tea-swilled, burnt-toast mornings.

In my Japanese dreams, I glide through Tokyo's electric nights waiting for the sun to rise. I am old, serene, patient. I have seen many things. Many beautiful things in my Japanese dreams, but I have yet to see the blossoms fall.

*

My world is street-lit and red-bricked.

Wet, fag-butt-littered, chuddy-splattered streets drift by as I'm bus-shook to work.

Dumped out, spewed into an industrial estate land, I'm fag-gasping into the factory that owns my soul, shrinks my aching Western heart.

Days.

Day after day the same. The same day. At work, I hum a little tune. *In Dreams.* At work, I work, I smile, I talk, I work, smile, talk. The same talk. Day after day.

Hello Peter. Hello Peter. Hello Peter.

These are the people. The only people in my life. They walk past with their faces, any face. Just faces on bodies. Walking past in blue overalls. This is the conveyor belt. These are the days of our lives. Hum a little tune. Shall we talk about the weather?

Break. Fag. Tea. Yesterday's conversation repeated, repeated, repeated. *Hello Peter.*

My work is important. My work is vital. I stand for twelve hours, three days a week. I often work four, sometimes five days, but always twelve hours. I stand next to faces that walk and talk and work like me. I bend, hunch, cramp, and ache over the belt that never stops.

My work is important. My work is vital. We are sorting prawns. For twelve hours.

Lunch. Fag. Greyish-limp-lettuce-thin-wet-bread-plastic-cheese-sandwich. Fag. Tea. *Hello Peter.*

The clock is my enemy. Hateful. On the belt, it takes hours for minutes to pass. This is my life. Ten years? Twenty? Thirty? All on the belt. At hours for minutes. What else is there? Nothing. Nothing except my Japanese dreams.

Hours for minutes, for twelve hours, for three, four, five days a week, for thirty years. On the belt. Work is important, is vital, is over for one more day. *Goodnight Peter.*

I arrived in darkness. Worked the belt under artificial light. I travel home in darkness. I will not see the sun until summer.

Bright lit bus, dark out window, dull orange city, fly by, fly by.

These are only faces on bodies hunched up beside me. Movement is good. The throb of engine takes us home. Nodding.

Tired.

*

The sun rises over the three great Kanzakura trees of Shinjuko Gyoen.

*

Tired like my street.

Hunched terraced houses elbow each other; they are stack-leaned close and closed curtained snug. The people are higgled and piggled on top of each other. No space. Closed streets. No space to breathe, to live, to dream. Houses full of faces, faces on bodies.

Some of the houses might be homes.

My house is small, walled, neat, neutral. I like the doors

closed. The fridge empty. The lights low. The blinds drawn. Shut down tight. It is a house.

I shovel trayed convenience into my silent mouth. Get smacked out on cheap TV dreams and DVDs. *Yojimbo* or *Yokubou, Sanjero* or *Shall We Dance? Rashomon* or *Rhapsody in August,* which *Nihon* tonight?

TV-tired eyes narrow, almost close, but I will watch the news today, so I can talk about yesterday's news tomorrow. The belt is always waiting.

Everything is switched off. I climb dark stairs to a cold, one-toothbrush bathroom. In the bedroom, I fold dirty clothes; fold clean clothes and fold back bedclothes. Everything is switched off.

I lie, straight, precise, ready for the belt. I stare into darkness, stare into a lifetime of single-bed nights. Hours for minutes.

I will deny myself my dreams. My Japanese Dreams. They are too bright to bear.

Tired. Tired.

*

Even for an old man, it is a short walk from Shinjuku Gyoen Mae Station to Shinjuku Gyoen. On a sunny, mid-March evening, it is also a pleasant walk. As always, I sit by the three great Kanzakura trees, next to the tearoom here in the traditional garden.

There is a carpet of pink blossoms around the trees, but these are not fallen blossoms. No. They are too early to be fallen.

I am watching a parakeet. It is a very happy bird. Yellow-green body, red bill and long tail. Plucking the Kanzakura from the tree, one after another, its bill picking and pecking at pollen-swollen blossom.

This bird and its many brethren are not native, no the parakeets are – *Gaijin-san* – escaped pets. While I, old and native Japanese, have still not seen the blossom fall, they pick and peck and make a fake fallen carpet of pink Kanzakura.

I leave the park, turn my back on the Parakeets. I will seek another kind of beauty.

Shinjuku streets at night: neon, streaming with youth and purpose, busy busy, *moshi moshi*, beeps and sirens and faces marching by, all blurs, and me an old man. Serene. I stand and watch and am fulfilled.

I do not go home. Instead, I watch Shinjuku life pass by. People moving together remind me of wind over summer grasses, in my mind, I paint calligraphy, haiku by Bashu, in Kanji.

Before dawn, when the morning night is at its darkest, its coldest, for a beat, just a heartbeat, Shinjuku slows to its lowest pulse. I close my eyes, breathe deeply.

Soon it will blast and blare again, be walk, don't walk with salaryman morning rush, but I will not be there. I have timed my walk back to Shinjuku Gyoen just so.

I will watch the sun rise above the three Kanzakura trees. There are no parakeets. I am old and I am serene. I have seen many things, but I have not yet seen the blossoms fall.

I kneel, patient like a Sensei.

Pink, the blossoms fall. One by one, a beautiful, slow-twirl fall full of seppuku grace.

But these are not blossoms. These are not Kanzakura. These are prawns falling from a tree. *Hello Peter*.

*

It's dark when I awake. It will be dark when I walk into the factory. It will be dark when I leave. It will be dark for twelve hours, for three, or four, or five days a week for the rest of my life.

I throw back the bedclothes, rip open the curtains. Sit back on the bed. Look out of the window into the street-lamp orange dark.

I pick up the telephone, dial.

'Hello…it's Peter. No, I won't be coming in today.'

Why do we do what we do, instead of what we want to do? Why?

'No, I'm going to sit here until the sun rises.'

When do we decide that tomorrow is too late?

'No, I won't be in tomorrow.'

How long can we wait?

'Or ever.'

Where are our lives going?

'Japan, don't know how long.'

They are short you know – our lives. Haiku short.

'Goodbye.'

Jethro
Ellen O'Neill

Ol' Jethro, he's tall as a grizzly and twice as ornery. Like to died the first time he walked in my door, stooping so low his nose scuffed the floor, beard like a broom sweeping it clean, just so's his head wouldn't bang against the top of the door frame. Would've pulled the whole house down if he did that. He'd come in, all scrunched up like, stuffing himself into my ol' comfy easy chair like it's a toy one – you know, like in little Addie's doll house, the one her daddy Joe made her when she turned six. Just before Joe died, that was. Anyway, that's what he looked like, Jethro, when he'd come to visit – a giant in a doll house. Had the bellow of a lion been done wrong – least got his tail stepped on. Yep, tall as a grizzly and roar like a lion, that man.

One night he comes over, crams himself into my little cabin of a house and decides to smoke a ceegar big as a log outta my woodpile. Heck, bigger! Uses one of my logs, straight outta the fire, still flaming like a match – uses it to light that ceegar of his. Fills the whole place with smoke each time he lets out a drag. My little Addie comes outta her room where she's been sleeping deep as water in a well. Sees him, eyes go wide as saucers, stops straight in her tracks and just stares at him, standing stiff as oak, 'fraid to move an inch.

Next thing I know, my boy Tommy comes in the front door yelling that the horses are so spooked they've kicked right out of their stalls, and he's sure there's something awful bad out there. Well, Jethro he jumps up, hits his head and pops it straight through the roof, shingles 'n all, rips the rest off, steps out of the house and, grabbing Addie and Tommy, stuffs them in his pockets, one on each side, and runs out to meet whatever's out there.

I mean, I swear this man by now was twice as tall as when he walked in my door. Or maybe I just felt awful small, so scared I was. I dunno.

But I know this. Ol' Jethro runs past the stables – yells to me 'They're safer with me Kate, you take the horse!' then tells the young'uns to hold tight to his beard, don't let go. Finally he lets out a yelp so loud it cracks two trees in half, splits them straight down the middle, honest to God – and takes off at a lope into the forest. I throw myself on my mare and we gallop for all we're worth just to try to follow them. Now, I'm hearing trees crashing down, big redwood I mean, not just scrub oak or pine, and noises – cries and screeches ugly as Hell on a Saturday night. I'm so scared my whole body's shaking. But I keep on going and my mare she don't fail, and together we leap over the fallen trees and mess of branches, 'til suddenly the night goes silent, and all I can hear is my heart thumping like a jackabilly in my chest. It's pitch black and not a sound in that forest, not even a jaybird crying sentinel for its brood. We slow to a crawl 'cause we got no place to aim for.

Then – you won't believe this now, I swear, but it's true – I hear this sweet little song coming from the west, toward the hills. A lullaby it is, one like my mama used to sing to me. And Bessie and me we just go for that sound and what do you think we found? Ol' Jethro looking big as a mountain, setting on top of a grizzly tall as two buildings, that ol' bear laid out like a log, dead as stone. And Jethro he's cradling my two young'uns in his arms like they're new-borns. Comforting them he was, singing them to sleep. The sound was so sweet, me 'n' Bessie, we just got on our knees, her first, then me, and wept. You ever seen a horse weep? No, neither me, 'til that night. Then we just curled up against that great bear of a man, and let him sing us to sleep too, same as the young'uns. Sweeter music I never heard, like all the heartache just oozed outta me, and left me fresh and new. That's how I felt the next morning.

There we were, Tommy, Addie, Bessie and me – and even the body of that ol' grizzly laid out stiff as ice. But no Jethro. Never have seen that man again.

But oh, I keep hoping – looking for his face when I scan a mountain range up close, or when the sky goes black as ravens' wings. And sometimes, when I hear a bird sing real sweet, I think that's him.

Antique Shopping
Lennart Lundh

There comes a late-November Sunday, even in the upper Midwest, when the world outside is just too beautiful for those of us who live here to stay cooped up inside. Golden sunlight dances through branches bare of all but the most tenacious leaves. Grass bends a bit in a southerly breeze. Birds and fowl halt their migration for a while.

Carol decided we should spend this gift of a day shopping for antiques. She wanted to find just the right occasional chair for our recently remodelled living room, and knew exactly what style of framed mirror would work above her dressing table. Having been married better than twenty years, I left thoughts of brats and the Packers unspoken while I found a light jacket and the car keys.

Once away from the city, we took county roads out to Taintsville. It was a lovely drive through the rolling countryside and past miles of fields filled with soybeans and winter wheat, every bit as perfect as the day surrounding it. I almost yielded to the temptation to put the roof down on our old ragtop Caddy and pretend we were teenagers again, wind in our hair and no cares in our world. Too soon, it seemed, we reached our destination.

Taintsville is a good place to hunt for true antiques at realistic prices. It's an old farming community, by and large, with enough shops on the outskirts to make the search worthwhile without crowding and over-commercialising the process. On a day like this, much of the merchandise would be displayed outside, on gently sloping lawns and flagstone walks.

We'd combine a stroll in the sunshine with serious shopping.

Sometimes, Carol would wander from store to store, examining each piece of furniture in great detail and never reaching a decision. Other times; well, have you ever seen a dog pick a person out of a crowd without hesitation, sensing something that promises a perfect match? As far as chairs were concerned, this was one of those quick times. At the second store, she spotted a handcrafted early nineteenth-century chair tucked away on the corner of the porch, looked only once at the price tag, and asked me if it would fit in the back of the car. I knew I'd have to make it fit; it was coming home with us.

That settled, and the chair settled comfortably in the car, she said to me, 'Hey, sailor. Buy a lady a meal? Maybe I'll show you a good time while you're in town.'

'Well, blow me down,' I said in my best Popeye voice. 'I yam what I yam.' Such a cultured, polite invitation. Back when I really was a sailor, the bargirls were more likely to say, 'I love you, Joe. Let's go short-time.'

Carol laughed, and managed a fair Olive Oyl in return. 'Okay, Sweet Potato, let's shiver our timbers over to Ashley's and see what's on the menu.'

We lunched on pot roast with baby potatoes and sweetcorn, the kind of meal you wish your mother had known how to make. Ashley's coffee is even better than her cooking, and we used the small talk old marriages are known for as an excuse to have an extra cup each. Good weather, good food, good company. Such a fine day.

'Ready for more?' Carol asked, meaning following her around the remaining four antique shops.

'Lead on,' I replied. And so she did.

The mirror Carol had in mind wasn't in the third store, nor the fourth or fifth. I'm not sure why she passed on the ones she saw there; several seemed beautiful to me, and perfectly suited to my image of what would fit her needs, both practical and aesthetic. As we approached the last shop, I thought we might be out of luck that day.

'That's it,' she exclaimed, and hurried over to a mirror that leaned against a small dresser. I smiled at the child's delight in her voice and step. 'The dimensions are perfect for what I want.'

She examined the frame from just enough distance to take in its overall design. Satisfied with what she saw, she moved close for a careful look at the woodwork. A little character-giving distress would be one thing; major scratches, dents, or warping would be unacceptable. Her fingers ran over the surface, feeling for exceptional roughness, poor polishing, or the falseness of an unoriginal finish. I felt like I was watching a blind person investigate a new face, and she did in fact close her eyes from time to time, as if to allow greater focus on touch.

When Carol was done looking at the front and sides, I pulled the mirror away from the dresser so she could give the back an equally thorough going over. Once she was finished, I leaned it back again and stepped away so she could examine the glass.

'No chips or scratches in the silvering,' she reported. 'Come over here and see what you think. I'm guessing there's a very attractive couple in the mirror.'

I stood next to her, on her left, and looked.

'Um, what a shame. There must be a flaw in the glass. I can see me,' I told her, 'But not you.'

She didn't answer immediately, but shifted her weight from one foot to the other and then back, all the while looking intently at the mirror. 'That,' she finally said, 'is strange.'

'You didn't tell me you had vampire blood in you,' I joked.

'Trade places with me.'

I moved to stand on her right side. 'Okay, so the mirror has vampire blood in its family.' Now I could see her reflection but not my own.

'That is a shame. Do you think we could replace the glass? The frame is exactly what I hoped to find.'

I moved the mirror and examined the back. 'Nope. This is the original glass, from the look of things. Probably never removed after it was placed. Change the glass and the value of the piece goes right down the toilet.'

'Yeah, I guess you're right.' She frowned, then looked up at the sky, where clouds were starting to bunch up to the west. 'Let's call it a day and get home before the rain comes. I found the chair, and fifty percent ain't a bad day's work.'

We both took one last look at the mirror. Carol shivered, though the air was still pleasantly warm.

She shivered again as I started the car.

'We'll get you warmed up as soon as the engine does,' I told her.

'I'm not cold. It's just that mirror. I've never seen anything so ... so weird. How did it do that?'

'I don't know,' I answered. 'I'm glad you decided to pass on it, though. I don't think I'd want it in the house. Sure you don't want the heat on?'

'Nah, but thanks, honey. I'll be okay.'

As we crossed out of town, Carol asked me, 'Do you know why it's called Taintsville?'

I did, in fact, but thought her story might be funnier than the truth. 'Do tell, please.'

'Well, you know this area was settled by Swedes and Norwegians, back when they mixed as well as oil and water. Whatever one group said, the other would say, 'No, it ain't.' After a while, people from other towns took to calling this Taintsville.'

I laughed. 'And you're going to tell me their soft-hearted children settled Missouri, saying 'show me' instead of 'it ain't'.'

'Exactly. You're a very smart man. Of course, you proved that years ago.'

'How?'

'You married me.'

*

We didn't get home before it started raining. The storm built rapidly, and caught up to us out on the two-lane, blacktop county road. Its speed was equalled by its intensity. Driving soon became a challenge. I remember turning the wipers to their fastest speed, and wondering if there was a safe place to pull off the road until the weather eased.

I don't remember anything between that and when I woke in the hospital. The doctors said limited amnesia is common in accident victims, especially where there's been either severe emotional distress or head trauma, and I'd suffered both. What they were telling me, I finally realized, was that I didn't really remember the crash. The things I saw in my mind's eye day and night were imagined, pictures drawn in great detail by the force of my survivor's guilt.

Carol's folks flew into Chicago and rode up here with my parents. The four of them took care of arrangements while I was still in an induced coma, and so I missed my wife's wake and cremation. I understand a lot of people came to pay their respects, more than she would ever have realised she could touch with her life. They saved the ashes for me to scatter over the Pacific Ocean she'd loved so much. And they held me safe, in both body and spirit, until I was ready to rejoin what was left of my world.

The area newspapers' accounts of the crash are generally clear. An oncoming pickup drifted into our lane on a curve, its driver blinded by the rain. Accidents happen, and I don't have it in my heart to hold my loss against him.

They're wrong on one point, though. She definitely was wearing her seatbelt. Neither of us would forget that all-important item. The police said it broke loose, allowing her to be thrown from the car.

And they leave out one thing. I would do anything, give everything, for her to have been on the left and me on the right.

A few years have passed, and with them perhaps a hundred Sunday drives along county roads to Taintsville. Sometimes the day is beautiful around my car. Other times the outside is as grey as the inside. The mirror is still there, unsold. And no matter how I stand before it, despite all prayers and supplications, I still see my reflection.

Daphne Changes
Joshan Esfandiari Martin

They met when she holidayed on his island paradise. Deedee and Tino. She loved him. He loved her. He said he would marry the sunburnt English girl. She was barely seventeen at the time; a young bride. But no matter. They moved to Coventry.

She had enormous eyes and sat with her hands on her lap. Waitresses came to and fro. She was at her usual table. Lexa, the beautiful one, saw her. Deedee was pretty, waiting patiently to give her order.

The café was bright, and informal, furnished in simple wood.

They smiled at each other. Lexa's face at Deedee's face. Deedee's tawny braids at Lexa's wholesomely red hair. Blue eyes. Brown eyes.

I like you.

I like you too.

Their skirts were so short, if the doorbell rang you could see their knickers. Lexa flexed her knees as she took the order. Deedee followed those legs as they went to the kitchen hatch. Full and beautiful calves.

*

After the honeymoon, Tino confessed he had no plans, so Deedee's father obtained a position for him at the waterworks. The other employees liked Tino. He had a funny way of talking.

Yeah, let's complete our shift nicely, yeah.

The accent was pure Mediterranean hokum. Deedee had been impressed by such things in her teenage years. She wasn't naïve. It was just that Tino had a certain stock charm. He was quite attractive.

Yeah, we're almost done it.

The lad seemed pleasant enough. Deedee's father didn't go in much for analysis. Why not marry his daughter, whatever her age? So when Deedee suggested she might have fallen out of love with Tino, he really didn't know what to say. Deedee did love Tino. It wasn't that. Only that her father was precisely the kind of blank board by which to check your echo.

Is it because of your illness? Do you feel this way because of your skin?

No, she said. *I keep mulling things over.*

Deedee's father was against mulling. Lately retired as a sewage supervisor, *mulling* to him implied blockage. When the shit wasn't hitting the fans properly. When it couldn't be sluiced to the bacto-vats. Then it would sit in the pipes for days, *mulling*. On a professional level, he believed the townsfolk should put as much distance as possible between themselves and their own dejected brown. His emotional views were much the same. *Otherwise,* as he said, *it can attract 'seafood'.*

*

She scratched her scalp. Her husband lay snoring. Half Greek, half Turk; wholly Cypriot. And very hairy. His name was Konstantino Dertilis. She was Daphne Dertilis. She was Deedee. In the middle of the night she sat bolt upright. Her husband dreaming dreams, his large hands resting on her thighs like the paws of some esoteric bear. There was a circular hum somewhere. A secret piece of house at work. An extractor maybe. Phasing with his snores.

*

With Deedee in mind, Lexa had lately been doing things in the bath. She wanted to tell her *I have a girlfriend!*

Deedee pointed to Lexa's top.

I like your blouse.
They let us wear our own clothes.
I wish I had your legs.
You have great legs, I can see.
Deedee beamed.

Lexa took the order, then took her curves and gracious manner to the kitchen hatch, watched all the while by Deedee. Deedee had something to tell her as well.

*

Dr Carr raised his eyes. The dryness and soreness were progressing. Now it spread down her back. He talked about psoriasis. The creams and ointments had no effect. Patches of skin had become hard and discoloured. Now it was starting in other places…

Have you had a smear test?
Smear?
Do you visit a gynaecologist at all?
A smear?

He took some surgical gloves from the drawer. He took off his jacket. She had a remembrance of a childhood feeling. Of going along with something, without knowing why.

She lay motionless, 'til his head reappeared.
I'll make out a prescription.
He put the gloves in the bin.
You can get down now.
How? she thought.
He leaned back and flicked open the stirrups.

*

Dough was nice. Kneading it and pressing it against her skin, she found it soothed the dry blotches on her wrist. Tino complained. He kept finding slivers of hard skin in the bread, like wood shavings. In the later stages of her condition Deedee took to encasing her shins in wet pastry. Tino said she was going crazy, but the irritation was so intense she would happily have bought her clothes at a bakery, if only it might help.

*

At night she would have vivid dreams. Being baked whole, en croûte, by her husband.

*

In between shifts at the café, the staff stood about smoking. Sometimes they played poker, placing bets with condiment sachets. Brown sauce for ten. Sweetener for twenty. Going all in with a fistful of vinegar. While her ointment was being made up at the chemist, Deedee came to see if Lexa was around.

A young Australian told her:

She's not on afternoons. She's already gone.

He was attractive in a dolphin sort of way. Made all priapic by the distance from his homeland. *Funny girl*, he thought. *All pigtails and girlish clothing.*

His proposition was unexpected. Her nubile dishabille was aimed at a single certain young woman. She hadn't thought of the collateral interest it might arouse. Her personhood was so tentative and imprecise.

I'm sorry, she said, *I couldn't possibly.*

*

She used a blob of coarse toothpaste down there. Minty and granular. Imagining herself and Lexa topless. On a speedboat. Their bare legs intertwined. Tensing. Eroto-stretching. As Tino slept beside her, she made compressed weepings, little computer noises, coming beneath their shared duvet.

*

…And you can check all you like, but at the end of the day no-one is going to show you how to shave like your dad can.

He rummaged through the medicine cabinet, pulling out rusty tubes and Christmas soap, placing the odd article on the side of the bath where Deedee had her trouser leg rolled up. Her bare knee was heavily mottled. The skin on her ankle was peeling yellow. Her father started lathering a badger brush with all the slowness of a panda making cake.

Why this one?
Things were done differently in those days. Less perfume.
It's old?
Before I met your mother.

He began to apply the foam to his daughter's leg. Up and down – long strokes as if priming a wall. Deedee watched his silence and care.

Try that.

She took an upward stroke with the blade. He furrowed his brow.

Maybe start with down. His poor child's skin!
It stings.
Why not leave off shaving for a while?

But Lexa… Lexa and her lovely legs…

Deedee continued with delicate motions. A sheaf of rind dropped from her calf into the bath.

*

And there was Tino, rubbing oil onto his wife's back after supper. Fine violet capillaries weeping through the skin. Wondering if it would make her scream, if he reached round and grabbed her tits? Rough hands massaging her sensitive back, and suddenly a tactile dimension was lost to Deedee. She asked him to stop, and went to stand topless in the garden, drying her back in the subtle evening sun. The cooling grass like prickly fudge between her toes. The vegetation turning dark drawing-room green. The sun went down. And with Lexa in her thoughts, her head vibrated something old and mythic with all this, as Tino's broken sprinkler pissed moronic arcs through the Etesian breeze.

*

Her father came to Tino with a box of cigars. He was concerned.

…Yeah, and if I said I was NOT concerned as well, I would be the liar. Like your Prime Minister.

Tino exhaled smoke.

Deedee's father was beginning to dislike the way his son-in-law spoke. There was a hint of menace in his non-identification with the premier of this, this country.

You are worried about my daughter then?

The Doctor's medicine is pointless.

At least stop her shaving.

This is a good cigar.

Tino didn't like hairy girls.

*

Lexa tried to seem nonchalant.

The girl at table seven was asking after you.

She let her eyes wander over to Deedee's ankles, those winsome attributes that excited her most. The Australian was more obviously staring at Deedee's t-shirt, bralessness being a feature he personally held in some esteem.

Hot damn she's a little minx ain't she!

Deedee's knee was really itchy.

*

Tino blew a smoke ring.

She stood in the sun for two hours yesterday. It helps, she says, but I fear ultraviolet.

Yes?

She doesn't have my olive skin.

Her father felt a geometric segment of racism rotate within his marrow.

Daphne is too fair. I say again, she does not have olive skin.

With that, he spat some tobacco strands across himself.

*

The end of summer was marked by winds. Tino decided

to run the marathon that coming spring. Deedee stood over the percolating coffee, waiting longer, longer and longer for him to return from jogging, waiting for him to come home and somehow snap her out of it.

She avoided the café. There was barely a palatable patch of skin she could now show. She felt morbid. Stiffening.

*

Lexa was downcast. Without the slight sexual stress of Deedee, her waitress work was tedious. Her underwear got duller. Her skirts grew longer. She had no-one to demonstrate herself to. It was the Australian who eventually pointed out such coyness was pointless. The contours of her body, however clothed, were enough to (as he somewhat creepily put it) *advertise the specials.*

By autumn it was complete. Daphne stood in the garden shedding leaves. Fusiform, copper leaves similar in colour to Lexa's hair. Eddies of wind jostled up impromptu sculptures with the dead foliage. Now a head, now an abstract, then dissipating and re-emerging as something else. She shaded a bank of acacia. All her branches were strong and new. Her father slaked her with a watering can, sometimes with his tears, examining her trunk to find some semblance of her eyes within the distribution of knots and crevices.

The breeze made her talk. The remaining leaves flittered. But it was fleeting, incomprehensible poetry. During the evenings, a pussycat often sat upon her boughs.

And at night, fresh-sweaty from his evening run, Tino would come out to the garden and rub his salty palms all over her bark. Sometimes ripping off a piece, or wrapping his legs round her trunk and pressing himself against her.

She had grown tall in no time, but her shape was not graceful as before. The puzzle was, how could a laurel grow in such a place as this?

Candyfloss
Maria Kyle

Used to be, every other night I saw her. Sometimes every night. How'd I know it was night? Everybody dreams at night, don't they? Night-time was for her and me and the banal monsters and the uncanny clowns and the people you know with the faces you don't. *Carnevale.*

So yeah, every few nights. The dark would come out like a fox from the shadows and so would she. And there I'd be, waiting for her. Always.

There were some bizarre scenes going on back then. All sorts of weird shit with Escher hotel corridors, strange meals that refused to be cooked, and mice, for some reason. Fucking mice everywhere: underfoot, overhead, swimming in the stews and slumping out of the soufflés, skittering down the walls like rain down a windowpane. One time I even lay back on this hotel bed only to find the pillow stuffed with mice – warm, soft, squirming. I never did get the mouse thing. But they went away eventually, and we could concentrate on each other.

Describe my relationship with her? What exactly do you mean by that? What, where and how often?

It wasn't like that.

Jesus, I don't know, what should it have been like? What's anything between a man and a woman like? Who am I, Sigmund Freud?

Yeah, she mentioned him. Why wouldn't she? She's an educated girl.

She just seemed that way. Articulate, you know? Soft-spoken.

Yes beautiful. Of course beautiful. Isn't everybody, in dreams? Everybody you love, anyhow.

*

The first time. OK.

It was a tunnel. A dark tunnel – wet, warm, kind of like a sewer, but no smell. Can you smell in dreams? I never could. Not womblike, not really, more intestinal. A dim orange glow spilling around the corner. It wasn't frightening, no, just … unfamiliar. I'd hurt my leg somehow, had to crawl, though there was room to stand. It was big as a tube tunnel, this place. The blood ran warm over my leg like bathwater. I knew it hurt but I couldn't feel the pain. There's no pain in dreams either. Except –

I didn't hear her behind me. What with the splashing, the dripping from the ceiling, I had no idea she was there, let alone so close, until she grabbed my leg. I felt her fingers close around my ankle, cool and clean like spring-water, and I panicked. I jerked my leg, tried to kick her away. She could have been anything. You know what it's like when dreams go bad.

She said my name.

I don't know how. How do you know anything in dreams? You just know.

I stopped. I twisted over. Her face was pale in the tunnel light and her hair hung wet around it, like she was fresh from the shower. I couldn't see her eyes but she was smiling.

Like a kid. Like a child with a present. Like she just saw her best friend for the first time after a long summer vacation. That's how.

She said my name again. I looked down and the leg she was touching, the wound, it wasn't bleeding any more. It was like I'd never even been hurt.

'Jesus,' she said, 'Is that really you?'

*

The tunnel. That was an old dream, one that could turn on a dime, turn bad. We got out of there fast and didn't go back. We tried hotels, sure, but we never could reach each other at the end of those looping corridors. Or else I'd lose my way back to the bedroom, barge in on wrong rooms full of strangers.

The mansion was better; I think she saw it in a TV movie once. Neither of us knew our way around. Secret passages, dust everywhere and cobwebs like candyfloss. Sometimes the dust became mice, too. Gave me the fucking creeps. But even though we got lost, got dirty, at least we did it together.

We eventually decided that open air was the key. That way you can see things coming, whatever they are. There's always somewhere to run. So we settled on meeting at a fairground – well, sometimes it was a fairground, sometimes a park or a playground: it depended on the night, on the dream. But always the same bench. Old, heavy, ornate, maybe Victorian, with wooden slats worn smooth and chipped dark-green paint.

I can see it now, so vivid; see the names carved into it. Some of them were decades old, some of them so new wood flesh was still bright in the scar. All different letterings, different angles – different alphabets, even. Like everybody had scratched their love into that thing at one time or another. Some of the names looked like when school kids etch their desks in exams, some were done with real craft, real attention to detail. Some were as basic as it gets. An initial, another initial, and in between them, a heart.

Whose names? Ours, of course. They were all ours.

We'd meet there and go. Anywhere, wherever she wanted. Wherever she could dream of.

Yeah, that was a good time. Dreams so good you don't want to wake up, you know? That's what she said to me. That she didn't want to wake up. And I didn't either. Want her to, I mean.

*

She confided in me, yeah. I didn't mind. I liked to hear what she did when she was awake. And I think it comforted her, to tell me. Let her let it go. A lot of shit with work; her ex, the depression, all that. She didn't need that. Especially not when she was asleep, when we were together. That was our time.

A few times she had anxiety dreams about work and I had to step in. Her boss tried to follow us around the fairground, but I lost him. Once he jumped out in the Tunnel of Love, dressed as a flamingo, so I tied his neck in a knot and turned him into a boat for the next couple. She laughed and said thank-you.

'Don't thank me,' I said, 'It's your dream.'

She kissed me then. It was like the sparks you see behind your eyelids when you can't sleep. Fireworks in the velvet void.

'It's our dream,' she said. 'Ours.'

*

Why would I talk about myself? I was happy enough just listening to her.

I thought I made her happy, too. But then she didn't come for a long time.

Hard to tell. Weeks? Let me count the days. I lost count.

When I saw her again she looked different somehow, white and thin, light-starved like a plant. It was a park that time, I remember. We sat by the duck pond. There was a picnic blanket and a hamper but she wouldn't eat.

She said they'd put her on new drugs. For the depression. There were side-effects. Loss of concentration, loss of appetite, even in dreams.

'It's the pills,' she said. 'I sleep all the time, but these days I hardly ever dream.'

That was where she'd been.

She looked so sad when she said it. Or maybe I did. The ducks drifted on the water like ships in mist.

Of course I wanted her to come off it. Of course I did.

Of course I didn't say anything.

*

The last time was a long while after. She'd come back once or twice, but the dreams were strange and pale, like old black-and-white movies, like something photocopied too much, and so was she.

She said she was doing better. In her waking life, that is. Coping.

What did I say? I said that was good.

We walked through the fairground, her hand cold in mine. I bought her candyfloss, but it didn't taste of anything. She said she didn't think she could see me any more. She wanted to, but the drugs kept her away. Like a mist she couldn't find her way through.

And she smiled.

Like a kid that's just broken a toy, that's how. Like saying goodbye to her best friend for the long summer vacation.

*

No, I don't want to move. I'm fine here. With the ducks and the carousel and all. Of course I can't see them now, but I know they're there. Just out of sight, just through the mist. Just like I know she is.

I'll wait. What else have I got to do?

As long as it takes. I owe her everything. She thought me up in the first place, after all. Her dream-boy. My dream-girl.

I know she'll come back. When she gets her head straight, when she doesn't need the drugs any more. One night the mist will just melt away like candyfloss on your tongue, the dark will come out like a fox from the shadows and so will she. And there I'll be, waiting for her. Always.

An Account of Six Poisonings
Nichol Wilmor

My sign was the pestle and mortar. My knowledge was roots and seeds, vines and leaves, bulbs and berries. I was a grinder, a blender, a crusher, a mulcher; I was a master of tubers. I mixed the tinctures and measured the powders that might cure or kill. (A single grain may be the difference between health and death.) Mine was a calling. A position of trust. I was the court's poisoner.

No more. My poisons are at hand but they are seldom employed. What I was I was, and what I am I am. I snore in warm corners. I slumber in a feather bed. I shuffle between here and there. If someone speaks, I cock my ear and pretend to deafness. If someone points, I squint and shake my head. My sign is a bent back, an elder stick, an idiot grin. Why do I play the ancient pantaloon? A poisoner has many enemies.

Ladies. Gentlemen. You have asked me for an account of the six poisonings. I will tell you the story, but you must know that it is a dangerous tale which never can be spoken of or shared. Have you taken my meaning? Then I will proceed.

*

– Their father was a loathsome toad.

Queen Utrica had an earthy way with words. The high-born have no fear of low speech while we who serve them search for gracious phrases or sweet ornaments. But I will try to emulate my mistress and speak as plainly as I may.

– He was a brute. As a husband he had nothing to commend him, she said. Nothing except his manliness. His great manliness. His considerable and undeniable manliness.

Queen Utrica sat for a moment lost in her memories of amatory battle.

– Yes, I wept at his death, she continued. A tear or two. No more. The wonder is that he died peacefully in his bed.

Here I will confess that I loved Queen Utrica. Humbly, wholly and devotedly. As the loam loves the trowel. As the worm loves the rose. As the living love the dead.

– Life was less beastly without him, said Queen Utrica. Much less beastly. I hoped my sons might be better men than their father, but I found I didn't like either of them.

The Queen sighed deeply.

– I wasn't made for motherhood, she said.

How I adored her.

– Hector and Cyril! What mistaken names we gave them. Hector was to have been a hero but he was as limp as a wilting lily. Pale, frail and feeble.

Although, it should be noted, something of a scholar. He excelled at poetry and music. (Mathematics was too vigorous for him.) At a young age, he retired to a single tower in a far corner of the castle grounds. There he wrote verses and played a zither while standing at a high window that overlooked a rose garden. Hector was never seen with a sword in his hand while his younger brother, Cyril, was seldom seen without one. Cyril was a roaring child. Fury-filled and certainly no scholar. His tutors were too terrorised to teach him either to read or write. Pain was Cyril's music; oaths were his verses. A horrid boy. But his father may have loved him.

When the King expired, it might have been argued that Hector, the first-born, should have succeeded to his throne. But it was an argument no one was willing to pursue. Cyril had spent so much of his youth cutting things off (arms, heads, legs and the like) and running things through (mostly guts and gizzards) that it was wise never to disagree with him.

King Cyril's coronation should have been a grand affair but it ended abruptly when the King felt it had gone on long enough. He had business to attend to, he said.

After slaughtering his rivals at home, he cast about for enemies abroad. The neighbouring kingdoms of Indium, Gallium and Thulium were conquered and despoiled in quick succession. Hugo Hairshirt, Edgar the Improbable and the Margrave Elector of Shining Badgers all surrendered their territories. (They were beheaded.) As was a catholic collection of chamberlains and chancellors. (Their heads were set up on poles.)

Prince Hector escaped his brother's savage ministrations and stayed untroubled in his tower; playing his zither, composing his verses and looking down from his high window on the rose garden below.

– I wonder, Queen Utrica sometimes asked, if I should have liked daughters any better.

I will permit myself to suggest that the Queen's opinion of her daughter-in-law, Rosalind, provides the answer.

– A slight, simpering creature, said Queen Utrica. I don't know where Cyril found her. Cowering in the cellar of some smouldering castle, I suppose.

Anyway Rosalind adored him. I can only speculate that he must have inherited his father's great manliness. After the perfunctory nuptials that united King Cyril and sweet Rosalind, there was a discomfiting lull. Indium, Gallium and Thulium had been reduced to rubble and there was no one left to fight. Thank God, then – if this isn't impious – for the Great Turk's blasphemy and the Pope's crusade to save the Holy Kidney. If he'd known about him, King Cyril would have set out to fight the Great Turk on his own, but his geography was shaky and it was handy to have the Papal map-reader to guide him to Constantinople, Aleppo and beyond. Thus it was that King Cyril left his kingdom for – as it transpired – seven years.

Queen Rosalind was distraught.

– A weepy, willowy girl, said Queen Utrica. I should have liked to snap her in two.

Rosalind took to walking in the rose garden, tearful, wretched, inconsolable. And, from his high window, Prince Hector watched her.

Despatches from King Cyril received at court told of battles, massacres, marches, sieges, trophies taken, prisoners slaughtered. Glorious triumphs in the cause of the Holy Kidney. We all hoped – although we did not admit it – that the Great Turk would continue his stubborn resistance. What we did not want – with the exception of Queen Rosalind, naturally – was King Cyril's return. Nor did we want him dead. Were King Cyril to be killed, chaos might be unleashed. A hundred clans and factions would twitch to life and – like reattached limbs – writhe and wrestle to take his lands. No, we needed King Cyril to be living. But not here.

Is not God good? This was our thought when first we heard the news that King Cyril had been captured by the Great Turk. It seemed an answer to our prayers. He lived – but far away in a deep dungeon. If we had known that the Great Turk – a chivalrous gentleman – had not in fact confined his prisoner in darkness but permitted him to wander through the luscious foliage and sweet fountains of his courtyard, it might not have troubled us. Although it should have done.

For a period, life was blissful. Harvests were good. Taxes were collected. Our lives at court could be enjoyed to the full. Rosalind, it is true, remained in her state of misery but now she was joined in her walks around the rose garden by Prince Hector who had descended from his tower to commune with her.

And then disaster. News reached us that King Cyril had escaped. Or – as we were later to learn – his escape had been effected by Fatima, the daughter of the Great Turk. She, it seems, had spied the prisoner walking day after day in her father's gardens and fallen in love with him. It was an unlucky turn of events. In a month or two King Cyril – accompanied by Fatima who, naturally, was now his lover – returned to his kingdom.

If you have read the chronicle, you will know what happened next. The official history is most touching. Fatima, the Great Turk's daughter, loved King Cyril as much as any woman could, while Rosalind's joy at her lord's return was such that she happily forgave her husband's love for his saviour. She, too, loved Fatima, and Cyril loved them both. He had no wish to choose between them. And so he sought a dispensation from the Pope to take a second wife which – in recognition of his service in the matter of the Holy Kidney – was granted. Cyril and Fatima were joined in holy matrimony and shared their bed with Rosalind. A loving trinity.

Ladies. Gentlemen. You must know that what one reads should not always be believed.

Nonetheless, King Cyril was a much-changed man. Whether he had been chastened by captivity or civilised by the Great Turk, is not for us to judge. And although he didn't learn to read or play himself, King Cyril could now be seen with his head in Fatima's lap while Rosalind sang sweetly or read verses of her own composition.

(Prince Hector had returned to his tower.)

If Rosalind frowned, King Cyril, resting beneath fragrant Fatima's soft bosom, saw nothing.

*

When Rosalind approached me, I sought Queen Utrica's counsel.

– Matrimony is a sacrament, said the Queen. It is your duty to restore propriety.

The stems of powdered monk-eye picked at dawn served Rosalind well; and Fatima died in frightful agony.

King Cyril, it seems, had favoured the Great Turk's daughter above adoring Rosalind and, although much reformed, his course was clear.

When King Cyril approached me, I sought Queen Utrica's counsel.

– The King is the agent of the Almighty, said the Queen. It is your duty to serve him faithfully.

The rind of ground angel-toe picked at noon served King Cyril well; and Rosalind died in frightful agony.

Prince Hector, from his high tower, saw all. The murder of beloved Rosalind was more than he could bear.

When Prince Hector approached me, I sought Queen Utrica's counsel.

– The heart's cause is sacred, said the Queen. It is your duty to worship at love's shrine.

The bark of crushed hermit-nose, picked at dusk, served Prince Hector well; and King Cyril died in frightful agony.

There was an interlude when it seemed Prince Hector might now descend from his tower in order to ascend the throne. This was, of course, unthinkable.

– Regicide and fratricide are offences against Nature, said Queen Utrica. It is your duty to ensure that justice is done.

The crust of sliced virgin-spleen, picked at night, served Queen Utrica well; and Prince Hector died in frightful agony.

Queen Utrica's rule was harsh but fair – well, harsh – and all was well. But then – as if for the first time – Queen Utrica seemed to see me. Her loyal servant. Her devoted slave. The court's poisoner. And I sensed that she was troubled.

I spied her walking in the rose garden, surveying roots and seeds, vines and leaves, bulbs and berries, and I, too, was troubled.

The husk of sieved poet-brain, picked day or night, has always served me well; and Queen Utrica – it pains me to confess – died in frightful agony.

*

This is an account of the six poisonings. Ladies. Gentlemen. I ask you to raise your glasses to poisoners and their melancholy profession. Drink deep. Drink long. That is good. Ah. You have been counting? The fragrant Fatima. Love-lost Rosalind. Cyril. Hector. And my beloved Queen. That's five poisonings, you say. Drink deep. Drink long. Flakes of baked phoenix-tripe are odourless and tasteless in a cup of wine or ale. Drink deep. Drink long. Did I not tell you that this was a dangerous tale that can never be spoken of or shared?

Free Cake
Peng Shepherd

Earlier this afternoon at 3pm, the head of my Assistant Director of Communications exploded. The incident shut down production for at least 45 minutes, while the rest of the Communications Department waited for the Cleaning Crew to remove the biological matter and sterilise the office to working standards. Total collateral damage was calculated at one computer terminal, three computer monitors, the all-in-one printer machine, two blazers, two blouses, and one pair of trousers (the two managers seated nearest to him). It was an exceptionally messy episode.

After the Cleaning Crew leaves and my team returns to work, I close my door and sit at my desk, staring down at my hands. I have to find a new Assistant Director of Communications now, a task which is not easy. The now-former Assistant Director of Communications, the exploded one, was excellent at his job. No one else in the Communications Department has the same amount of experience or expertise. I will have to interview external candidates.

But worst of all, I have to reset our DAYS WITHOUT EXPLOSION! counter back to zero, which puts my department in last place, and gives the lead to the Sales division, with 52. I step back and look at the row of DAYS WITHOUT EXPLOSION! counters on the wall in the staff kitchen and sigh. Even Finance is ahead of us now.

*

At home over dinner, my wife asks me about my day at work. 'My Assistant Director of Communications exploded today,' I sigh, stabbing a stalk of buttered asparagus.

'Oh, that's too bad!' She clicks her tongue. 'We had one last week too.'

'Hm,' I mumble, and stab another asparagus. They are slightly overcooked. The bloated spear hangs limply as I lift my fork into the air.

'Honey?' I look up and realize she's staring at me, brow furrowed. 'What's the matter?'

A drop of oil slides to the tip of the stalk and falls, plinking against the plate in a pale yellow pool. 'It just really caught me off-guard,' I finally say. 'I thought … I thought he was happy.'

'Oh honey, you can't blame yourself. These things are so individualised.' She reaches across the table and pats my hand. 'There's nothing you could have done. Even if you tried to help, he still might have exploded anyway. Some people are just prone to it. Pow!' She flicks her fingers open next to her head, miming the burst. 'You know?'

'I know,' I say, and look back to the asparagus wilting on my fork.

She goes back to eating. 'Don't worry. I'm sure it will take you no time at all to find a new Assistant Director. Everything will be back to normal before you know it.'

I put the drooping stalk in my mouth. 'These are great.' I try to smile.

*

The following day, the office is quieter than usual. Voices are more hushed, papers shuffle more softly. Even the morning announcements seem more muted. The Assistant Director's empty chair looks strange, a blank spot in the sea of occupied desks. The Cleaning Crew did a good job; everything has been wiped down and disinfected, ready for the next Assistant Director of Communications, and all of the re-useable property has been lined up at the top. They even managed to save his paperclips, painstakingly cleaning each one. You can't tell at all that just yesterday they were covered in blood and grey brain meat.

I work my way through the stack of reports I have to approve, carefully examining each one and stamping the upper right corner with my red PROCESSED stamp. This is normally the Assistant Director of Communications' job, but until I'm able to find a new one, someone has to do it. I flip through the pages of each one, scanning the text, and then flip back to the first page and press firmly down, to make sure the ink doesn't smear. Flip, scan, flip, stamp. Flip, scan, flip, stamp.

After finishing 25 reports, I stand up and stretch, clicking the box on my desk. The light comes on, and a 15-minute timer and calming music begins. I stroll back and forth in front of the window, rolling my head in a circle and shrugging my shoulders as I stare out at the city. Normally I don't take one of my fifteen-minute breaks so early, but for a week after an incident, everyone's account is automatically credited with one extra per day. I continue stretching, following the routine I learned during orientation, specially designed by scientists to decrease the chances of explosion. I close my eyes, trying to feel the stress 'melt out of me', as she put it. 'Breathe deeply,' the New Hire trainer's voice says soothingly, 'And feel the stress melt out of you.' I feel nothing though.

The box beeps quietly to let me know I have only 5 minutes left. I finish the stretching and relaxation routine and look out the window again. The sky is overcast, a whitish-grey vacuum above the landscape of steel and glass skyscrapers. My eyes drift across the buildings, looking into the million tiny windows that dot their faces. I wonder how many other people in them are exploding right now, splattering their brains across their computers and covering their desks in pieces of head.

I try not to think about it, but I can't help it. I wonder

what it was that sent my Assistant Director over the edge. You always hope it's a big thing, something really worth it, like losing a major contract or getting passed over for a promotion, but I heard about one guy who exploded after coming back from a three-day weekend and turning on his computer to find he had 500 emails. He took one look at the screen and detonated. Or about this other woman who set the staff kitchen microwave too high, and burned her lunch. Melted the plastic container lid right down onto her low-fat pasta. She opened the door and saw the smouldering mess and just blew.

My box beeps again, and the music cuts off abruptly. I sit back down and reach for the 26th report.

Between reports 41 and 42, I visit Human Resources to close out the paperwork for my exploded Assistant Director, and submit an advertisement for his newly available position. I have modified the package slightly, adding an additional hour of flex-time per week and increasing the daily lunch break allotment by 5 minutes. The Head of Human Resources raises her eyebrow at the changes, but enters them into her records without saying anything.

'A shame,' she sighs when she has finished, her chair squeaking as she turns towards me. 'He was such a productive employee.'

I nod, watching the blubber in her neck quiver as she talks, rippling like waves through an ocean.

'Well, luckily we have a birthday today.' She clicks her red pen and gives me an even smile. 'A thirty minute break and free cake should do wonders for morale!' She turns back to her computer. 'I'll make the announcement just after lunch.'

I take the elevator back to my floor and return to my desk. Everyone looks up as I enter the room. I smile pleasantly at them, trying to exude friendliness and calm. They all lower their heads and go back to typing.

I work diligently for the rest of the morning, trying to clear the pile on my desk. Flip, scan, flip, stamp. Flip, scan, flip, stamp. When the lunch bell rings, I wait in line at the microwave, holding my plastic food container. Inside is leftover steak and slightly overcooked asparagus from last night. I put my container in the microwave and turn the dial. They are probably nearly gelatinous by now.

I return to my desk with the steaming container and continue working, my red PROCESSED stamp in one hand and my silver fork from home in the other. Flip, scan, flip, stamp, bite. Flip, scan, flip, stamp, bite. The asparagus squishes between my teeth as I chew, soft like pudding.

Midway through my 84th report, the intercom clicks on and a scratchy recording of the birthday song blares through the office. The Head of Human Resources cuts in over the music, announcing that there is a birthday celebration in the staff cafeteria for a Mr. Harrison Wheeler, from Sales. I come out of my office and watch everyone's face as they listen. Some look happy enough, but I can tell that others are disappointed, probably expecting the rest of the afternoon off, or one of the other typically offered perks that HR doles out after an explosion, to try to prevent further occurrences.

When the intercom clicks off, we all get up from our desks and shuffle into the elevator to go down to the staff cafeteria. Everyone faces front, staring up at the ticking red number above the doors. No one speaks.

The elevator dings, and the doors slide open to reveal the cafeteria. Several other departments are already there, lined up near the centre table for a piece of cake. My team joins the wait, lining up in almost the same order as their desks upstairs. 'I hope I get an end piece,' one of them says.

I look around, trying to figure out who Mr. Harrison Wheeler is. Then I see him, at the far end of the room, near the cake. He is slumped awkwardly in the stiff-backed chair at the head of the table, a paper cone birthday hat affixed to his balding head and a long cake knife in one hand. His face is blank, a limp mask of skin and hair.

'Happy birthday, Harrison!' the Head of Human Resources sings merrily, chin wobbling, and sets something shiny down on the table in front of him, nearly knocking the red bow off the top with her thick fingers. 'It's a special stress reliever, engraved with your name on it! The CEO had it moulded especially for you, so it fits to your palm perfectly. You just hold it in one hand and squeeze! Isn't that great?'

Harrison looks down at the engraved stress reliever, his face still blank. His eyes drift up to the party, to the crowd of employees milling aimlessly around the staff cafeteria, eating cake and sipping powdered fruit punch out of flimsy paper cups. Our eyes meet across the room.

'Harrison?' The Head of Human Resources leans closer, eyebrows furrowing across her bulbous forehead. 'Is everything okay?'

For just a moment, his expression changes. Oh no, I think. Then his head explodes.

*

The birthday party is over. Half of the Cleaning Crew is upstairs with us, clearing the newly vacant Sales desk, and the other half is still in the cafeteria, mopping up the remains and bathing the Head of Human Resources, who was completely covered from head to toe in bits of Mr. Harrison Wheeler.

I sit at my desk again, staring down at my hands.

Suddenly one of the Cleaning Crew trudges through my door. He bends over slowly, looking down at my desk through the tiny plastic viewing window of his hazmat helmet, and slides a piece of cake on a paper plate next to my keyboard. 'Free cake,' he says, his voice muffled through the full-body suit.

I stare down at the dessert, surprised. It's chocolate, with chocolate frosting, and not a single speck of brains on top.

'Fork?' He holds a white plastic utensil out to me with one rubber-gloved arm.

I take it from him. 'Uh. Thanks,' I finally say.

'Enjoy,' he nods once, giant helmet bobbing, and plods awkwardly off towards the other desks, cradling three more paper plates in his hands.

I watch him go, and look back to my cake. It looks fresh and moist. I have to admit, the Head of Human Resources did a remarkable job of blocking Harrison's explosion with her gigantic body. The sweetness of the chocolate reaches my nostrils.

I don't know what else to do. I sigh and stick my fork in.

Worms' Feast
David Mildon

I was tired.

Aching, sluggish and extremely hung-over. A succession of dive bars and dank hotels in piddling European towns had not quenched my thirst.

London was a bust. Our friends were all, in fact, hers.

My feet were treading cobbles. Cobbles meant picturesque. Picturesque meant tourists. I lurched down a small road, looking for somewhere which didn't speak English. It's important to stretch the budget when you're low on funds and have forgotten which city you're in.

I blame the euro. Before, you could get skull-fuckingly drunk and still know your approximate location by emptying your pockets the next morning and looking at the shrapnel. Now all you've got to go on is a continent.

The street turned to tarmac and the shop windows grew dirtier. I was clearly heading in the right direction and smiled at the thought of a drink. I was soon rewarded by the wrought-iron silhouette of a foaming beer mug swinging above an archway.

I crossed the road, faintly aware of some hooting and honking from irate motorists and stood under the arch. This was indeed not one for the tourists. In front of me was a tiny courtyard. A consumptive tree stretched towards an elusive shaft of natural light in one corner, while in another old and broken chairs were piled high. Beyond, there was a door panelled with small squares of sickly yellow glass. I couldn't tell whether there were lights on inside.

The door opened to my shove with a judder and a bang.

The whole room was a long rectangle, each side lined with wood panelling and mirrors. Trestle tables and benches ran along each wall, with another length of tables down the middle. The bar was open, insofar as the lights glowered dimly and a man stood behind the taps in one of the far corners. I was not quite his only customer, the dubious honour of getting the first drink of the day having fallen to a morose-looking black man halfway down the left hand row of tables. He nursed a large glass of beer and stared fixedly at himself in the mirror.

I sat down on the other side of the room from him, back to the wall. This was what I needed. Even the barman was perfect, wearing an apron and the sort of thick, curving moustaches that few people have the balls to carry off. He came to the table and waited. I gestured at the beer my solitary companion had before him; the message seemed clear enough, as our host walked back to the bar and began pulling me a drink.

It was warm and quiet, just a gentle drumming of rain to break the silence. When the beer arrived, bill slipped beneath the glass, I drank deep, mixing last night's excesses with today's new beginnings. It didn't seem like the sort of place where people were easily offended, so when the first wave of sleep hit me, quieting the angry voices behind my eyes, I stopped resisting and let the undertow drag me down.

*

I was awoken by a jab in the ribs and a grunt. As my eyes focused I saw that someone had shoved onto the bench next to me. Looking beyond his shoulder, I could see why. The room was heaving with a great tide of men.

A roiling, deep-bass hum filled the room, along with a smell like drying mud. Occasional shouts of recognition came as newcomers entered through the left of two doors by the bar. I must have come in the back way. Each arrival seemed to have several old friends among the assembled drinkers.

The men were filthy, their clothes rapidly composting into rags. Dark red-brown stains and dirty bandages made me feel that perhaps I should drink elsewhere. I took a handful of coins out of my pocket and looked at the bill.

All that was marked on it was a stamped line of black numbers:

1 2 8 4 7 9 3 3 1

The man sitting across from me noticed my confusion.

'English?'

Typical; try as I might, my country of origin seems painfully obvious the world around. I nodded to my new friend with a grimace. His smile was reassuring, at odds with the army greatcoat that dwarfed him.

'First time?'

I assented and waved my bill with a gesture of helplessness that he seemed to understand. He looked at the paper avidly.

'Black means no charge for first drink.'

This was odd, but the whole bar had a strange atmosphere, the crowd of men smoking and drinking with single-minded ferocity.

'You want something more for drink?'

I shrugged, not sure if I should stay, but unwilling to be rude, especially in the face of an offer of drink.

He smiled broadly, waved a paper with a short number in red ink stamped upon it and rose from his seat. He hefted a collection of belts and pouches up onto the chair he had just vacated. Among his belongings were an aluminium canteen, a bayonet in a rusting scabbard and a pair of stick-grenades. The more I looked around, the more I sensed that I was at odds with the rest of the company.

Increasingly uncomfortable, I realised that this had not gone unnoticed and struggled to avoid the gaze of several newly-interested patrons. One particularly imposing drinker with a shock of blonde hair and a livid scar across his throat ambled towards my table.

'English?'

I nodded, eyeing the broad slashes in his grenadier's uniform.

'Crecy, Spion Kop, El Alamein,'

I nodded again, at a loss. He did not strike me as a man to argue with.

'First t…'

His next question was interrupted by a hand on his chest; my drinking companion was quietly gazing up at the interloper, a friendly smile on his lupine features. Looking down from a head taller, the blonde juggernaut pursed his lips and trudged away,

'Sorry for this.'

'That's quite alright. Thank you for the beer.'

'Just need the red numbers and it's always free.'

A sudden hush fell upon the room as the landlord walked over to the two back doors and wiped down a dusty blackboard. Soon every man in the room was clutching a little scrap of paper like my companion's, each with a line of red digits stamped upon it.

As the chalk squeaked out 10 lines of numbers, the room filled with perverse cries of jubilation as men realised they were not amongst the winners. Once the landlord replaced the white stick, ten men hefted packs, belts and canvas bags and moved towards the back of the room.

As each passed beside the bar, the landlord handed out fresh uniforms in blues, greens, browns and reds, his words to each man drowned by a rising tattoo of glasses upon table. As the shouting and thrumming from each corner reached its climax, the men walked one by one through the right hand door of the pair.

I looked across the table to where my new acquaintance seemed unaffected by the cacophony; he hacked at a dry sausage with his bayonet.

'The door?'

'You need red for that.' He twirled his yellowed paper between his fingers.

'Where does it go?'

'Everywhere. Wherever men fight, or have fought, or will one day. As I said, everywhere.'

Our eyes met, his smile less forced than mine.

There was a draught of air as the left-hand door swung open, and through it limped a short youth dressed all in black, a tricolour band on his arm. He walked to the bar where a drink was waiting for him and gingerly removed his glasses. They hung at an angle, both lenses broken in a spider pattern. He took a long draught and rubbed his face. Taking his beret in both hands, he wrung it out like a cloth, unconcerned as a slow trickle of red liquid spattered the floor at his feet.

'Whatever you think you have lost outside, there is always better in here.'

His smile was still warm and open.

'I should be getting on…' My hand went to the black stamped bill, only to find it enclosed by his gloved fist.

'Many homes. Many lives. So many, you'll forget this one.'

I glanced around, watching the fug of shared sweat rise.

When I looked back to the table, a red-stamped scrap sat beside my own. Looking from hand to arm and up to face, I saw his smile was gone.

'Change? With me. Give me your pass. Take mine.'

I hesitated, hearing the voices of every army in history.

'Try something new. I need to rest. You can have a new life. Lives.'

I breathed in, smelling the sickly aroma of decay. Slowly, carefully, I shook my head, hand closing on my black printed piece of paper.

With a cry my new companion jumped to his feet, snatching up his chair as glasses, weapons and neighbours skittered away from him. The chair swung up and down towards me.

*

A watery light woke me. A quick check of my pockets told me that none of my possessions had wandered in the night. I opened my right hand, and there, framed by the red welts of dug-in nails, nestled the piece of paper bearing nine black digits. Around me the bar sat empty, so I pulled myself up and shuffled towards the yellow-paned door.

As I emerged into the half-light of dawn I came face to face with the barman. I raised my bill towards him, as if to ask how I should pay. His answer was a curt nod before he returned to tossing the fragments of a broken chair onto the pile.

After a moment's indecision, I walked through the archway and quickened my pace as I set off in search of the train station.

The Museum of the Future
Richard Meredith

I wanted to do one last crazy thing before I settled down and started popping out kids and painting the picket fence, so I thought I'd give the Museum of the Future a try. Space-tourism was kind of last decade, so when some acid casualty told me about the Museum at a loft party that Christmas, it sounded perfect. I thought about it hard for six months, then I kissed my sleeping husband Jack, took a Valium, got in the car and drove to the place the guy had mentioned.

It was a deserted street corner someplace in the unfashionable part of the meat-packing district – deep badlands, a long walk from the nearest subway, loomed over by decommissioned warehouses and dying streetlamps. I sat there for a half-hour or more before I saw a soul. It was a good thing Jack kept a fifth of rye in the glove compartment, or I would have got real cold and scared, real quick.

There was a quick tap on the car window and I buzzed it down. A tall thin black guy leaned in suddenly and I jumped. He twisted his head sideways, widened his eyes and smiled at me. It was dazzling.

'It's OK, Molly,' he said. 'You're here for the tour, right?'

I nodded.

'Well come on then,' he said, 'I'm the curator. Your guide.'

I stepped out of the car and took his extended hand. Stupid, right? What was I thinking? How did I know he was the right guy, not some crazy street person? I'll tell you why. For one thing, he knew my name. For another, it was dark in my car and it was dark on those streets, but wherever that guy looked it was lit up bright as Christmas. He had sort of little headlight beams coming out of his eyes.

That's what *really* sold me.

*

He led the way to a warehouse like any other, except – just like the guy at the party had said – it had a door like a stable door, half open at the top. My guide didn't open the bottom half, he just climbed over and then helped me do the same, tearing a couple nice holes in my pantyhose in the process. I didn't ask why. I guessed it must be important.

'You got the money?' he said.

'Sure,' I showed him; he flicked through and pocketed it.

'Sorry it's kind of a lot,' he said. 'Inflation, you know?'

I shrugged sympathetically.

'You OK with the other part of the fee?' he said.

'Sure,' I said. He motioned me to a long metal table and I lay flat on it, face down. He took a little metal box, about the size of a paperback novel, from his jacket. I lifted my shirt and he placed the box on my lower back. It felt warm and weird.

'Give it ten years and they can grow me another one anyway,' I joked.

He frowned. 'More like seventeen,' he said. The box sucked itself to my skin and buzzed briefly. When he lifted it again it seemed heavier, and sloshed slightly. There was no pain, and no blood – at least, none that I could see.

'Would you like to see the first exhibit?' said my guide.

*

The Museum itself was a vast, abandoned warehouse piled to the roof with every kind and colour of trash you could ever think of. Old furniture, newspapers, scratched CDs and cracked DVDs and worn-out electrical junk; clothes outgrown, toys and gadgets abandoned, broken jewellery, faded photographs. I especially remember the cellphones, thousands of them, old and battered even when they were some razor-thin, ultramodern design that probably hadn't even been thought of yet.

'What the hell?' I said. If I was just going to be shown the contents of a hundred dumpsters and told that this was the future, I wanted my goddamn kidney back.

'Chill,' said my guide, 'I've found your stuff.' He flicked his torch eyes over to where a freestanding glass case, about the size of an icebox, emerged under his gaze from the darkness. A sign on it said 'Exhibit 1'. It had something inside it, oblong and tattered, yellow-white. As I approached I saw it was a newspaper, a local rag from somewhere in Colorado. Jack always said he wanted to move back there to be near his folks.

It had an article about me becoming Mayor of some little town I'd never heard of – the first woman and the first non-Coloradan to hold the office. There was a bumptious campaign photo of me and Jack raising our fists in victory. Apparently I was a former lawyer (check), a tireless worker for local charitable causes, and a mother of three. The last two didn't sound like me, but I guessed that fifteen years bored out of her skull in Long Bend, Colorado would probably make a mother and a charity worker out of anyone. Weird thing was, in the picture I looked really happy. Old (I guessed Botox would be hard to come by in Long Bend) but happy.

'Cool,' I said. 'Next stop, the White House, right?'

My guide shrugged. 'I only know as much as you do. This stuff was all I could find.'

I turned to face him. He lowered his dazzling eyes and my shoes shone, bright and disembodied, in the dipped beams.

'What do you mean, all you could find? Find where?'

He gestured behind him at the mountains of trash.

'You're kidding me.'

'No.'

'It must have taken years.'

'Yes.'

'Why?'

'I look all the time, for plenty of folks. Whoever's been, whoever's coming. It's amazing what you turn up. I never stop looking. It's my job.'

'But I only decided to do this tonight. I only even heard about it a few months ago. How did you know I was coming?'

He pulled a grubby leather diary out of his pocket and showed me today's entry. My name, the time and year, and the names of the cross streets where I had sat were scrawled in faded black ink that looked to be years old – maybe decades.

'You had an appointment,' he said.

We moved on slowly to the next exhibit.

There were unpublished books – paper and download – and bank statements and animatronic postcards from people I hadn't met yet. We looked at the drawings my unborn kids had made, from grade school through to art school, the holes from the thumbtacks still visible in the corners of the paper.

'But this is all stuff people have thrown out,' I said to the curator. 'What kind of mother am I? Why would I throw these out?'

He turned his head away. In the distance, another glass case glinted and flashed. 'Everything fetches up here in the end,' he said.

*

I stood at the last case watching the clip over and over. The recording was broken, futzed or messed up somehow so only a few seconds could be viewed. The quality was real good, better than TV, although it looked like it was being filmed from a camera somehow mounted in Jack's shades, because the picture kept jerking upwards as he pushed them up his nose.

There was a bulky thirtysomething woman who looked a little like me in the foreground, encouraging a couple of gawky kids, maybe six and eight years old, to do some kind of gymnastics. They were dressed in weird little matching playsuits that seemed to be made out of Spandex or Teflon or something. They did handstands and walkovers, and then one of them did a clumsy half-somersault, and everybody clapped.

A couple of heavyset older guys wandered into shot, holding drinks and laughing. My sons. My daughter and my grandkids and my sons. The sun was clear and high and the yard looked tidy and urban, nothing like how I imagined Long Bend. Where was this? When was this? There were murmurs of congratulations, brotherly ribbing and something about a barbecue. The last person to speak before the recording snapped out was Jack.

'I wish Molly was here to see this,' he said, and not like I'd gone to the store for milk, either.

I turned to the guide.

'I don't know,' he said. 'There's no date on the recording. It's a long way away, is all I can tell. That's not good enough for you?'

'No,' I said.

'I don't know,' he said again.

*

That was a while ago, but I never forgot, because it all happened like he showed me. Jack's transfer to Colorado. Three kids, two boys and a girl. I do work for charity, now, in between the housework. It's a medical charity based at the local hospital, run by doctors from the University at Boulder. I campaign for stem cell research to grow human organs from scratch. I truly believe the lives we will save outweigh any number of ethical problems.

It's been ten years. Seven to go.

I save, and I invest my savings wisely. That newspaper my guide showed me had a few interesting advertisements in it – I didn't recognise the names, but I remembered them. Jack's not sure how much is in my nest-egg, but by the time I'll need it, I'll have more than enough. Sometimes I think about the curator, rooting through all that stuff, day in, day out, looking for a photo or a tape or a newspaper article. A medical report, or a letter – or an obituary.

I tell myself I'm not being irrational. Who wants to open a book and not read the end? And who knows what else he'll have found by the time I go back? Like he said, he never stops looking.

Hollow Man
Rebecca J Payne

I'm the first to admit that I'm not always immaculately turned out. A little bedhead some days, a little unshaven perhaps. You know that. You've seen me around. But first impressions count, so I'd hate for you to get the wrong idea, sweetheart. This skin I'm walking around in ain't all there is to me.

*

Can I get you a drink? It's not a come-on, unless you want it to be. Something soft, then. A cool lemon and lime with a just dash of brown sugar. Cleans all the bad tastes from your mouth and leaves your palate wide open for whatever's round the corner. My shout. The barman here knows how to make them right for me.

You know, your perfume drew me to you. It holds the most delicate hint of apple beneath the higher notes. Like strolling past an orchard in the summertime; I can scent when the fruit is ripening. I once had a man for dinner who ran a family vineyard in the Dordogne. He could tell the moment the grapes were just right to be picked, pressed, transformed into something intoxicating. I learned a lot from him that night. I think I can learn a lot from you too.

But where are my manners? I haven't told you my name. It's Latrocutis. I know, I know, what were my parents thinking? Too busy to think it through, I guess. When I was young they fought like cats and dogs, or maybe demons and angels. Depends which way you look at it I suppose. But I haven't spoken to either of them in a very long time. To tell you the truth, they mellowed with age. They just don't come around this way too often anymore.

Your lip gloss is cherry flavoured. Even through the smoke I can taste it on your breath every time you lick your lips. Take another sip – didn't I tell you the bartender here is good to me? Knows me pretty well, better than most of the meatheads in this place. Look at them. Dozens of lost souls hurling themselves at each other to the same constant beat, all in the hope of making meaningful contact. Their desperation tastes like milk left too long in the sun.

But not you. I think you'd taste like the purest strawberries and cream. You seem unsteady on your feet – are you sure you're okay, Strawberry? Why don't you let me walk you home?

*

Here – take my coat. It's all right, I won't notice the difference – the whole of this world feels cold to me. Where I come from it's so hot that the air itself is on fire all day and night. And the stink of it sometimes! That takeaway across the street is cooking rancid meat. Can you smell it? It's like that everywhere back home. Rotten, foul, burning flesh. I don't know how I put up with it for so long before coming here. Hold on to me if you think you're going to stumble; I want to get you home safely.

You people don't know how good you've got it here and you're throwing it all away. When I first arrived I could drink fresh water from the streams and breathe in air that tasted of grass and sunlight. Now – now it's got the aftertaste of acid wherever I go, and you have to dig into mountains to find water you haven't tainted with your own filth. Listen to me, I sound like an old man. A very old man. But it's not all bad; up here I can still go for a walk with a beautiful woman down a moonlit street, and I can still taste the storm clouds moving in on the horizon. The sharp friction in the air, like the trace of hot spice in a Bloody Mary. He really gave you selfish people more than you'll ever know.

Do you work around here? Wait, let me guess: you seem to me like a nurse, or maybe a nursery teacher. I think you look after people who can't look after themselves. I've known men and women like that before; strawberries and cream, all of them. The kind of taste you sometimes just crave. Watch out for the drop in the kerb, Strawberry. Lean on me if you need to.

You see that drunk couple shouting at each other down the road – they were doomed from the start. You know how I know that? He's citrus, she's dairy. They curdle until nobody can stand to be around them anymore. Keep your senses open to it when we walk by them and you'll smell it too. It's always there, beneath the skin, the true taste of a person. I've just had a hundred lifetimes to learn to understand it.

You know the worst person I ever had for dinner? Out of all of them – the salad priests, the rare bloody butchers, the stringy street-corner drug dealers – the absolute worst of all was an actor. That man tasted of *nothing*. Jesus, I'd rather eat a dozen peppery housewives than another actor. Like tap water on Shredded Wheat. He'd spent his whole life being other people – sometimes I wonder if I'd taste that way.

I don't want to think about it anymore. I just want to breathe in your golden hair. God, please tell me you live nearby. I am ravenous tonight.

*

Your apartment is so cosy. I like the burgundy trim on the curtains. Maybe we should have another drink first? A glass of red wine, something full-bodied. I know you have some – you're that kind of person. Why don't you fetch it while I take a look around.

You have a lot of pictures of friends. Pretty vanilla-looking if you don't mind me saying. But the sword above the mantelpiece – nice touch. It's even real, isn't it? Family heirloom? Must be, the hilt looks old. Really old. You've got some musty smelling books, too. The leather spines on some of them are starting to crumble. Nothing lasts forever, I suppose. We all come to dust in the end. Did you bring the wine?

Huh. I've got to hand it to you. Your eye for detail is wonderful. The way you've matched the cream wallpaper with the silk cushions, the bronze light fittings with the fireplace – and you saw through to the real me, didn't you? The hollow man inside someone else's skin. You saw what no-one else could see. That crossbow you're holding even matches your eyes.

I never did find out you what you do for a living.

Heriot
Richard Smyth

I was born at some point in the nineteen-sixties. I'm English, I'm from the north of England. My parents – I'm of unknown parentage. I'm learning, slowly but surely. Everyone here has been very helpful.

'Do you remember it? Any of it?' Doctor Wainwright asked me this morning.

I thought hard. I did not remember. I shook my head.

'Nothing?'

'Nothing, sir.'

He smiled.

'You don't have to call me *Sir*,' he said.

They call me Heriot, which is what I call myself. We are agreed that I am Heriot.

As regards the other data, I accept them without question; without the least question. And yet –

When I was first asked, I replied that I was born in twenty-one-nineteen, in South Utsire Province of the United Kingdom of Scandinavia and Storbritannien. I replied that my parents were both architects, Ophelia and Hablot Sterne; I said that they were both alive and well and living in the Boknjaford archipelago.

My opinions in this regard were at first contested and then dismissed.

I am grateful for the doctors, who are reasonable men and women. There is another man here. Danny, he is called. I am not sure how reasonable he is.

When I first arrived here he engaged me in conversation.

This was before I had been briefed by the doctors. I told him the truth, as I then believed it to be.

'I am Professor Martin Heriot,' I said. 'In June twenty-one-sixty-three I, as the project leader at the Fysiska Institutionen at the University of Lerwick, submitted to an innovative treatment devised by our researchers.' I did not enter into detail: I don't think Danny would have understood the detail. 'It was intended,' I said, 'that I should achieve retrograde motion in the temporal plane.'

He gasped, and said: 'You mean...?'

There was a long pause. I realised that he hadn't the faintest idea what I meant. I told him that it had been intended that I should travel back in time. And that it appeared that that objective had been achieved.

He gasped again. I don't think that he is a reasonable man.

That evening, Doctor Wainwright and Doctor Hayward invited me to their office. I told them what I had told Danny. They, in turn, told me what I, at the beginning of this account, told you. Data based on physical examination and other research. I was born in the nineteen-sixties – and so on.

'Very well,' I said. 'I cannot, after all, corroborate my statement.'

They looked at me blankly.

Dr Hayward said: 'Pardon me?'

It seemed that they were unaccustomed to answers of this sort.

I said that, in a rational balance, the uncorroborated and unreliable evidence of my memory was very little, indeed, against the facts of the case: that I had been found wandering half-dressed and bewildered in the suburbs of Aberdeen, that I seemed in no sense to be out of the ordinary – that I was, in short, only an unidentified vagrant with an incredible story to tell.

Identification, photographs and a statement from the

President of the UKSS to the people of twenty-twelve had (I thought) been packed along with my person in the experimental capsule. But it seemed that they had not survived the treatment.

It seemed, I mean, that there had *been* no treatment.

'Extraordinary,' Dr Wainwright smiled.

Later that night, I sat at the barred window and watched the starry skies. I remembered that I had studied diagrams, beautiful diagrams, of how these skies would look. The diagrams, based on archive data, had been correct – but these skies were more beautiful than the diagrams.

Danny had come to sit beside me.

'People have to know,' he said. He nodded fervently. His gingery dreadlocks wagged.

'Know what?'

'That you're from the *future*, man.'

I shook my head.

'No, Danny. I'm not. I'm really not. I just thought that I was.'

He squinted, and rubbed at his right temple.

'You ain't going to believe,' he demanded, 'what *they* tell you, are you?'

I laughed. He hit me. I fell heavily on to the tiles. Danny was already blubbing an apology: 'I'm sorry, man, I'm sorry – don't tell them, will you? – don't send them after me, man.'

Danny is, like me, mentally ill.

What troubles me is that Danny, unlike me, is not alone. He is visited, at least once weekly, by his family: a mother, a sister, a brother. He has told them about me.

This is what troubles me. They – they who are not ill, not insane, not confined in a hospital but free to work, marry, drive cars, vote – they believed him.

It is aberrant beyond my capacity for expression.

Danny told me that they are going to take the story to

the newspapers. At first this didn't bother me; what sort of newspaper, I scoffed to myself, would report – as if they were news, as if they were fact – the delusions of an incarcerated mental patient?

But then I thought of Danny's family, who are not mad. They believed Danny's story. They believed – for no other reason than that somebody told them – that I was a man from the future. I fear that I don't yet have the measure of this world. I fear that the newspapers will believe them. And then where will I be?

Where am I now?

This morning Danny sat down cross-legged beside me.

'You can't, man,' he muttered. 'You gotta.'

I leaned towards him.

'Can't what? Got to what?'

'You can't let 'em *break* you. You gotta *fight* 'em.' He looked up, staring fiercely, and jabbed a finger in the direction of my forehead. 'You know, man. That's what counts. You know.'

I am afraid of Danny, since he hit me. I didn't speak.

'You've seen things,' Danny urged, nodding his head. 'You've *been* there, you *remember* stuff, don't you? Don't you, man? It's *in* there.' Again he jabbed the finger. 'And they can't get in there. Remember that, man – *they* can't get in there, it's *yours*. Don't let 'em in, man. Don't let 'em in.'

Now he tapped his own forehead.

'In here is what matters,' he said.

My jaw may have dropped open in astonishment.

In there, I thought, *is a diseased mess. In here, too.* Uncertain and fearful, I murmured something (perhaps only to comfort myself) about evidence.

'The only evidence I need,' Danny said, 'is what I see, what I hear, and what I know.'

I covered my face with my hands, for I could not contain my weeping.

I thought, once, that I lived in a time of consensus. Corroboration is truth. Reality is not a private property.

But I have woken from my madness and found this. A cult enslaved by the weak eye, the weak mind, the treacherous memory, the individual, the lonely and fallible one.

One man, I wanted to tell Danny, cannot know anything. But instead I only wept.

It's nearly morning. I could be wrong, I tell myself. Perhaps it is only Danny's deranged family that practise this deviancy; perhaps it's only by good fortune and subterfuge that they have evaded the attentions of the mental health authorities. Perhaps, out there, other people – perhaps all the other people – feel as I do.

If they do not then I will barely know how I feel myself.

I fear that they do not. I fear that newspapermen will shortly be crowding at the doors of the institute. I watch the old stars, which I learned from history books, fade in the sky.

I was born in the nineteen-sixties, I tell myself. I am of unknown parentage.

Hopefully, I will one day forget the things that I used to remember.

Touchdown
Christopher Samuels

I was born in a storm, somewhere several miles above the Atlantic Ocean. This was unexpected, to say the least, as my mother was only six months pregnant at the time, but so it was. She went into short, sharp labour in the aeroplane toilet during the in-flight movie (*Heaven's Gate* – she didn't miss much) and by the time the nuts and Bloody Marys were being handed around, I was squealing and squalling tinnily in the washbasin.

There were jokey, heart-warming articles in a number of newspapers, and a bit of debate about what nationality I was (it was a KLM flight from Amsterdam to New York, in international airspace), but all I got out of it in the end was dual Dutch-US nationality and a fascination with aeroplanes that led me to train as a pilot. And thanks in part to this, I haven't set foot on solid ground for the last seven years.

It's sort of a curse thing.

*

See, seven years ago, when I was just a captain-in-training on my first long-haul flight to Cape Town, there was a terrible storm over the South Atlantic. The aircraft was shaking, lights flickering, trolleys careening down the aisles, the works. I was only twenty-five and I didn't want to die. Well, nobody wants to die at any age, I suppose, but the will to live is considerably stronger when you haven't had nearly as much sex as you want or know you're capable of – when the world is your Rubik's cube and you haven't got bored of playing with it yet.

I handed over the control column and watched my co-pilot's nostrils whiten as the plane yawed and pitched. This got me worried. As a long-haul newbie I was well within my rights to be shitting myself in the midst of a sudden electrical storm; but Hanne, who had worked the Asian and African routes for twelve years, was ghost-pale beneath her peach foundation, and fingering her St. Christopher. Only then did I start to panic.

'We're going to be OK, aren't we?' I asked. She nodded greyly, but I could see her frosted lips moving in prayer.

'I expect you've seen worse than this?' I added, cheerfully. 'Hanne?'

Lightning crashed into a wing, and the port engine burst into blinding flames. Various alarms began sounding and half the instrument panel went red.

'Jesus Christ,' said Hanne, blanching even further, and crossing herself. The craft began to list and turn; I could feel the skewed g-forces pushing me out of my chair. I grabbed the control column and wrestled it, my hands slick with sweat, and through my head ran a mantra: *Jesus, Allah, Buddha, Jehovah, Beelzebub – just get us out of this alive and I will give you anything.*

Needless to say, that's something I now rather regret.

*

The passengers and crew have all got to know one another rather well over the ensuing years; well, privacy's not really an option when you have to spend the rest of your immortal life flying the unfriendly skies as a warning to other planes, dragging the lethal weather behind you like an ominous black comfort blanket. No aircraft that sights us emerges unscathed, although a few struggle back to an airport or landing-strip, to pass on the legend of the ghostly, blazing 747 that rides on a storm cloud, and heralds death and disaster to anyone who sees it.

Relationships form and dissolve and occasional fights break out, and I'm pretty sure that every adult on the flight is now a member of the mile-high club several times over –

but what else can we do? We've all seen the in-flight movies a hundred times. We ran out of peanuts, microwaveable meals and lemon-scented hand-wipes years ago, but still we drag on our unearthly existence. It appears that, as the living dead aboard a ghost plane, we have no need to eat any more, and no way to die.

Our sole entertainment has become watching others crash, explode and plummet to a longed-for oblivion, lit by the phantom firelight of our eternally burning port engine. People place bets on the manner of these unfortunate passengers' demise, or take pictures on their mobiles as the falling bodies plunge past the Perspex portholes. From the cockpit, Hanne and I can usually hear the desperate maydays of the crew on our radio, and that entertained us for the first few years, but after a while I switched it off – we can't talk back to them, and listening to their awful pleas and prayers gets repetitive and depressing after a time. They don't know how lucky they are: at least they aren't cruising the skies eternally, with no prospect of ever coming in to land.

*

And then, one day – the seventh anniversary of the Cape storm, as it happens – as we are surfing a hurricane above Nevada, waiting to intercept a northbound Airbus which has a date with destiny, my radio crackles into life.

'You're cleared to land, KLM0815, over.'

I don't understand. I bang the mike and stare at Hanne.

'What, over?' I flick the switch to open the comms channels to the cabin. I don't want anyone on board to miss this.

'You are cleared to land at Las Vegas. McCarran International airport, Runway Three. Shore leave, twenty-four hours, every seven years. If you – or someone you can persuade to replace you – aren't back in the air this time tomorrow, you die. Make the most of it. Over.'

And the voice cuts out again.

'Who the fuck was that?' gasps Hanne.

'I don't want to know,' I say, as I start to bring us in to land.

*

Vegas isn't a hard place to find all the things we've been missing during our seven-year stretch in the air. Booze and drugs are the two main items on most people's shopping lists, closely followed by sex of the anonymous, expensive variety, CNN, the internet, and a working phone line. Everybody wants to know what's happened while they've been away; wants to send messages of love and hope and hello and goodbye to their families. Everybody needs to decide, in their waking life of twenty-four hours, after the living death of the last seven years, whether they are going to get back on the plane. Maybe death would be better after all.

What do I do?

Well, I wander. I can hardly believe I'm back on land after so long in the sky – and while everyone else rushes lemming-like to the casinos, the brothels and the phone booths, I stand still in the towering lobby of the Luxor hotel and watch life blur around me. My parents are dead (in an air-crash, ironically, a few years before I got my pilot's licence). I've got no brothers and sisters, and nobody to miss me. I can do anything I want in this single, precious day. Problem is, I don't want to do anything, except maybe find myself a bar and a bed and a boy. Preferably someone who'll stay faithful over the next seven years until I get shore-leave again. Or even better, someone who'll swap places with me for my next tour. As if that's going to happen.

This being Vegas, I find everything I want in no time flat, and by midnight, Pacific Standard Time, I'm relaxing in the Mandalay Bay's high-roller suite with a gorgeous Texan called Jody and keeping a nervous eye on the ticking clock.

'You know this is just a one-night stand, right?' I tell Jody, as I chop up a few more lines of the grade-A coke my roulette winnings have bought me.

He doesn't look at me.

'Yeah, sure.'

'Not that I don't want to – you seem like a nice kid, you know?'

'So why not?'

What the hell.

'I'm kind of cursed. It's complicated.'

He snorts like I don't know the half of it.

'You're cursed.'

I get the sense he doesn't really believe me, and this makes me annoyed.

'Yes, I'm cursed, I'm fucking cursed, do you want to make something of it? You want proof?'

'That I'd like to see,' he says in his long, sexy Texan drawl.

'Well, tough. You'll just have to take my word for it. But trust me, it's pretty shitty.'

'Whatever.'

'What do you mean, whatever? I'm cursed, goddammit! Tomorrow night I've got to get back on a phantom 747 and spend the next seven years flying round the world heralding plane crashes! A little sympathy would be nice.'

Jody shrugs.

'You think you've got troubles? You're lucky, man. I've got pancreatic cancer and like six weeks to live.'

'Oh,' is all I can say to this.

And then I realise that if Jody wants to live, and I want to get off KLM0815, we can do each other a huge favour.

*

Twelve hours later I'm standing in the cockpit showing Jody the controls. Quite a few of the passengers and crew seem to have had the same brainwave as me and the seats are now filled with junkies and cancer patients, AIDS victims and transplantlisters and the very, very old: anyone, in fact, for whom seven years on a ghost plane seems like a good alternative to what they've got waiting for them down below.

Hanne's huddled in the co-pilot's seat, staring blankly at the artificial horizon. I guess she couldn't find anyone to swap with her – or maybe she just didn't try. She always was soft-hearted. When she called her husband he refused to believe it was her; he thought it was some sick prank. Everyone knows 815 vanished seven years ago, he said. We've moved on. Her son's in hospital and her daughter's getting married next week and she can't be with either of them. Jody and I try to ignore her.

'Well,' I say, 'it's mostly automatic, plus I'm pretty sure this bird can't crash whatever happens, but still – good luck man,' and I put out my hand to shake his. But he's staring in concern at Hanne. We've taken on as many supplies as we can and she's working her way through the vodka miniatures while they still have an effect.

'Is she OK?'

I think of Hanne's husband and children. I think of my own personal network of one, and then I surprise myself.

'Hanne,' I say. 'Go.'

She looks up.

'What?'

'Get out of here. Go on. Find your family. Take my free pass. Jody'll stay here and so will I. He can replace you instead of me. Ok?'

'But what about you?' she says, hope igniting in her eyes.

'Fuck it, this is all pretty much my fault anyway. Plus, what've I got to stay here for? C'mon, scoot. We're taking off in ten.'

Hanne hugs me hard, shakes Jody's hand, and wipes her tears away.

'You'll be OK?' she asks, and I shrug and smile.

As we make our ascent, breaking through the scrappy cloud cover and out into the black desert night, Jody leans over to me. He really is awfully cute. I start to wonder whether the next few years staring at that handsome profile is such a terrible punishment after all.

'Did I hear you say something about this whole ghost plane thing being down to you?' he asks.

'It's a long story,' I tell him.

'What the hell,' he says, 'we've got seven years.'

I glance at him and grin. Already he's looking healthier; the stasis of the curse is starting to work on him. Never grow old, never die – until next shore leave, that is. I flip on the cabin camera. The junkies and terminals in the cheap seats have all gone quiet, staring out of the portholes at the astonishing stars. Our port engine reignites with a soft *whump*, and we glide on into the dark.

What Does H_2O Feel Like to the Tadpoles?
Tom McKay

Like greasy algae they say, like the shock of the new – and we say, no, and, that can't be true. Like a thousand fine tendrils caressing your most sensitive parts they say and we blush because we find it awkward that the tadpoles should say such things – and we stare up into the sky until the bright sun burns our eyes. It's like having space and no space at the same time they say, and wiggle their little tails at us knowingly, like we should know what they mean – but we don't – we don't know what they mean at all and we think it is beginning to show on our faces. It's like when you wake from a dream but can't quite manage to move your limbs they say, it's like falling upwards, and we say ahhh and yes, and hmmm, and we stroke our chins like we understand – but we don't.

We reach into our pockets and jingle some loose change; we shift our balance from left to right and nod thoughtfully. We are trying to buy some time; we think hard, we think furiously – but to no avail, when we try to concentrate, other thoughts pop into our minds, other distractions, other avenues mislead us. The tadpoles are not convinced anyway; we are bad actors. They sense in our demeanour a degree of uncertainty and, kindly, magnanimously, they try again.

It's like a thick clean canvas on a cold tented night they say, it's like pulling the hood up on your jacket real tight – it's like a world of beads you can never part, it's like a fishy momentum, it's like cracking an egg cleanly onto a bed of flour – and then they reconsider and shake their heads and say, no, no, it's not like that at all.

We're not following, we say, exasperated, we don't understand – and those of them with small developing hands point at us questioningly. You breathe air they say, and we say yes, and inhale deeply and feel our chests expand; we stretch our shoulders back and blow out through our mouths loudly. We feel vindicated somehow. Well what is air like for you – they ask with interest, because they are inquisitive creatures, and always happy to oblige – and so we pause and hum and whistle and we flick some dry leaves into the pond.

It's like an atmosphere we say, finally, and shrug – though we know that's not what they want to hear – and they grin and look back and forth and then explode with laughter and their round little tadpole eyes bulge unforgivingly. That's not good enough they say, that just won't do! Think harder! they demand as they wiggle and dance beneath the oily surface tension of the pond. They do this to encourage us.

It's like a sort of 'tension' we say hesitantly – on our skin, the softest hair, the shell of a tortoise, it's like sleeping beneath a ceiling fan – and somehow they are not impressed, and we feel bad about letting them down. It's like the side veins on a green leaf we say, it's like storm clouds and wind, but we know it's not like the wind, the wind is too obvious and that's not what they want to hear. For a moment we think about vacuum cleaners and helicopters and hang gliders – but we think that's all irrelevant somehow.

It's like, it's like 'empirical data' – we struggle with a rush of bad intellect, and we push our glasses up high to the bridges of our noses – but we can't quite recall exactly what that term means and we know it. It's like science we say grasping, it's like religion, it's like prayer and philosophy – those things can explain it, but we don't quite know how they could – and the tadpoles can guess it but they are too polite to call our bluff, and so instead they blow glutinous bubbles which pop on the surface and expand little ripples out towards the edges of the pond.

It's like a ripple expanding we say finally, from nothing into something, and they stop wriggling and look over in our direction. It's like feeling satisfied we say desperately, it's like attachment, it's like love – and they nod their heads in approval, it's like language we say and they gather together in excitement to listen, it's like inevitability we say, as one tadpole with arms and legs and almost no tail at all pulls itself out of the water and slumps exhausted onto a rock. It's like growing old we say, and they look at us sympathetically and smile their tadpole smiles.

The Last Words of Emanuel Prettyjohn
Jonathan Pinnock

Alison Fish, midwife

He were a funny wee babby, that one. Came out of his mam with a head full of blonde curls and a big beaming smile on his face. Nary a scream nor a whimper: nothing. He just looked at me with them big round eyes, smiling. And y'know, I think all of us in the delivery room just stopped and stared at him for a moment. Then we caught each other and sniggered like we was kind of embarrassed.

It weren't a creepy sort of smile, though. It were a good little smile. It made you glow inside. Made you feel the world weren't such a bad place after all. Made you think there was hope. I wonder what ever happened to the little bugger.

Jack Hopkins, neighbour

I tell you what, as soon as I saw them move in I said to Doreen – remember, Doreen? – I said there goes our peace and quiet. Bloody thing'll keep us awake the whole time with its screaming and wailing because that's what they're like – aren't they Doreen? – waking up and wanting its feed and whatever else they do.

But the odd thing was we never heard a peep out of him. Quiet as a mouse he was, wasn't he Doreen? They only stayed for a year or two and then them foreigners moved in. We could tell you a thing or two about that lot, couldn't we? Oh yes.

Miss Jemima Philips, primary school teacher

Well, of course I remember him. Who wouldn't? He

wasn't what you'd call an ordinary pupil. When his mum brought him in and introduced him, he looked me firmly in the eye and slowly shook my hand. Then he smiled and I was taken aback by the sheer – I know this sounds really odd – by the sheer intensity of it. Does that make sense?

His mum took me to one side and explained he hadn't spoken a single word or tried to write anything during his entire life. They'd obviously had him checked out and he wasn't deaf or anything. He just didn't seem to want to say anything. He understood instructions perfectly and he was a very obedient child. But he was completely mute. I told her that we got all sorts there, and most of them turned out all right in the end, so not to worry.

Then she gave me this odd look, as if to say, you don't know the half of it. It took a few weeks of trying to get him to communicate with me before I realised what she meant. It wasn't so much that he didn't want to say anything. It was more that he didn't feel the need to.

Harry Philpott, schoolteacher (retd.)

Oh, I remember him all right. Bloody nuisance. Well, can you imagine it? A whole classroom full of kids, with me trying to get them to focus on getting their sodding GCSE coursework done, and there's moonface in the middle of them all just smiling beatifically like he's fucking Jesus.

If I'd been allowed to, you know what I'd have done? I'd have thrashed the little bugger senseless. Never did me any harm. But you can't do that sort of thing anymore, can you? Political correctness gone mad, that's what it is. World's gone bonkers, if you ask me.

Polly Wilson, classmate

We all thought he was a bit of a freak, to be honest. I

mean, we'd flick things at him and he'd just turn around and smile at us. Weird or what? But it was odd, because after a while we all sort of accepted him, and there was always a gang of kids around him. He was just a good guy to be around, I suppose. And he didn't half wind up that bastard Philpott. Drove the old git to a breakdown, apparently. That was just so cool. Yeah, Prettyface was good value just for that.

Simon Hornchurch, headmaster

Well, he didn't exactly add to the school's exam rating, did he? Although he did manage a GCSE in art. It was old whatsisname the head of English who had the idea, although it started off as a joke. We put his whole life up as a sort of conceptual art project. Got him an A*. I wonder if he realised what was going on. Strange boy. I often wondered if there was some kind of abuse going on at home, although he always seemed happy enough.

Of course, he didn't stay after his GCSEs, because there wasn't much he could really do, and we did wonder what was going to happen to him. So it was all quite a surprise when things turned out the way they did.

Statement of Edwina Prettyjohn, mother

We loved our son Emanuel deeply and I am as devastated by recent events as much as my late husband would have been. I would ask, however, that my request to be left in peace is respected.

Eric Jones, self-styled cult survivor and webmaster of silentgabrielisanevilbastard.com

Those swine wrecked my life. Before I joined them, I had a job. I had a wife. I had access to my kids. More than that, I had self-respect. But a year with them and I was a raving nutter, reduced to living on the streets. You would not believe some of the things I saw.

And that Silent Gabriel, he should be strung up for some of the things he done. Just ask him how much he's making out of this, next time you see him. But you won't get an answer. I guarantee you that.

Extract from interview with Stella Crumshaw, author of Cult of Silence: Emanuel Prettyjohn and the Quietness Phenomenon.

It wasn't Prettyjohn himself who set up the Quietness Movement; obviously, that would have been impossible. He was just the figurehead. The guy behind it all was Alex Templeman – or 'Silent Gabriel' as he would later style himself. Templeman was standing behind Prettyjohn in the queue at the dole office when they met. Prettyjohn was standing there just smiling at everyone and Templeman noticed that, instead of getting angry and frustrated with him, the people there rushed around trying to help. I'm pretty sure Templeman must have felt the power of the famous smile as well, because he wrote about the incident in a brief memoir shortly afterwards.

In this document, Templeman states that the meeting with Prettyjohn was the turning point in his life. He realised what was wrong with the world was not that we didn't talk to each other enough, but that we talked to each other too much. There was just too much pointless connectivity. At that point, he writes, I resolved never to say or write another word ever again. From then on, he says, I decided to Become Quiet.

When this memoir was posted on the internet, it had an extraordinary effect. The tired, the lonely and the needy all came to seek them out: Prettyjohn the new Messiah and Templeman his Evangelist. I don't doubt many of them got something out of it, some kind of comfort, because there certainly was something about the man. I know the one time I met Prettyjohn, I did feel some kind of inner glow, and I went away with a spring in my step that I couldn't really understand at all.

It wasn't long before they had to find accommodation for all the new members of the Cult – for that is what it had become. So it became necessary to raise funds, and this is where things began to get a little murkier. The easiest way to raise money was simply to ask all the members of the Cult to pledge a percentage of their earnings, and this is what originally happened; one assumes Silent Gabriel suspended his vow long enough to get the message across. The precise point at which this changed from being a percentage of all earnings to all their worldly goods isn't clear, but there were soon rumours of curious extravagances, Swiss bank accounts, money laundering and suchlike.

Harry Stump, proprietor of Southside Limousines, Ltd.

Lovely guy, Mr Gabriel. One of our best customers. Always went for the full pimped-out spec, never cut any corners. Always paid on the nail. Never demanded credit, never asked for discount. The perfect customer. Terrific guy. Great sense of humour, too.

Jodie Wellbeloved, former cult member

Well, it was a kind of weird time for me, y'know? I mean my life was, like, well, totally fucked, y'know? But those Quiet guys like turned it around for me, made me respect myself? Sure, I had to give them everything I owned, but like they said, money's just all about banks talking to each other, and when we're Quiet, we don't like need them to talk anymore? I mean, like, I didn't really understand what they were saying, but, like, whatever?

So every day we just spent, like, hours in the meeting hall just being Quiet and it was like really cool and sometimes Emanuel would come in and smile at us and everything would be like really groovy and we'd all smile at each other and feel really peaceful, like? And then sometimes Silent Gabriel would invite one of us into his room for some one-to-one tuition, which was all a bit weird. He had a rough beard, and I found him a bit gross, like? So I'm, like, doing Boo-dism now. It's cool.

Alex Templeman a.k.a. Silent Gabriel

Briony Fairchild, mother of cult member

I'm not saying that everything Eric Jones says is true. We have certainly had our disagreements, mainly in the area of presentation. I mean to say, some of the stuff on that website of his is completely beyond the pale. I don't know how he gets away with it sometimes. But let's just say that when all this blew up, I wasn't a bit surprised. Fortunately, when she joined, Tamara didn't have access to her trust fund and so the blighters haven't got their stinking mitts on that. Yet.

I just hope that Tam's got enough nous to work out which

way the wind is blowing. Apparently the bust up between Mr Prettyjohn and Silent Gabriel or whatever he calls himself was quite public. From what I've heard, he just sort of glowered at him. I didn't know he could glower. I thought all he ever did was smile, so it must have meant something pretty bad.

I've tried calling Tam on her mobile if only to say I told you so, but of course she hasn't got it any more, and she probably wouldn't answer me anyway. I do miss her awfully.

Inspector Frobisher, Northants CID

We have been trying to get a statement from any existing members of the religious organisation known as the Quiet Movement to cover the period on or around the 17th of June, 2011. I would, however, go so far as to say that there is, quite literally, a conspiracy of silence surrounding the place, and that all attempts so far to obtain said statement have been completely unproductive. Inquiries are continuing.

Mitzi Fantoni, emergency call centre operative

I was the one who took the call. It was a really strange voice. I said, 'Fire, Police or Ambulance?' as usual, but all I could get out of the man was a sort of 'Flthggggh' noise. I repeated the question, but the answer didn't make any more sense than the first one. So I said, 'Is there something wrong with you?' and he just said 'Ithkggggh poisggggggggh'. Of course, now I realise he was probably trying to say he'd been poisoned but I suppose if you've never said a word in your life before it's a bit hard to start with that.

So, yeah, I'm the one who heard the last words of Emanuel Prettyjohn. And I guess it was me that heard the first ones as well. Funny that.

Zwo
Alan Graham

'Eins Zwo' Acht Acht Zwo Sechs'

I can tell from the number that it's Krond. I move the phone an inch from my ear before he bellows his reply.

'Earthman Thomas! Are you still willing to help me out tonight?'

'Of course, when I've finished in the office. I know, I know, I did promise.'

'Yes. YES! Promise, Thomas. You need to meet me at six of the pm. This is an important promise, Thomas!'

'I'll be there, Krond. And I've translated those German letters you had, just bills and stuff. Nothing important.'

'Promise Thomas. Excellent.'

There was a huge pause as I could tell he was wracking his giant brain for the right word.

'Wunderbar, yes? Thomas. Wunderbar!'

He hung up. Suppressed laughter from the nearby desks told me my co-workers had overheard yet another loud call from my friend Krond.

I imagined the derisive whispers they were sharing: 'Does the Englishman think it impresses anyone to get calls from such a creature?' and 'Of course *they* would be friends.' My German was never quite good enough to work out exactly what they were saying, but I still got the gist of it.

I stood up angrily and tried to make eye-contact with the sniggerati. They locked their faces onto their computer screens and pretended I didn't exist. This was ridiculous. What did it matter that Krond was my friend? Krond, the Bulbous-Headed

Has-Been of the Hollywood B-Movie, once the monstrous star of Fifties alien invasion films; a creature who'd carried countless blondes in his giant claw-like hands back to numerous unconvincing UFOs. Did they think themselves so above it all, so untouchable?

Instead of meekly sitting back down again, I made my way to the stationery cupboard. I was glad it was empty; once again I could feel my loathing for my co-workers rising: I needed to be alone. I spent the rest of the afternoon avoiding my desk, counting down the minutes 'til I could escape and head over to Krond's place.

*

I could see him as I approached his flat, standing on the balcony – nine feet tall, three of those taken up by his enormous brain-shaped green head. As usual he was gazing down as men and machines efficiently took apart the Wall, piece by piece. He'd first come to West Berlin not long after it had gone up, finding the city, with its greater tolerance for the peculiar, a welcome refuge from his failing film career. I think he liked being witness to the Wall's demise.

'Thomas – I shall meet you at the car!' he shouted down. 'Posters? Do you think I should bring posters? Will there be fans, Thomas? I have pens!'

'It's an airport, Krond. No posters.'

'Yes. I'll bring some. Just in case.'

In the car, it was obvious quite how excited he was, and he prattled unceasingly as we drove through the streets. 'Did you hear, Melvous B. Hickney died? Now *there* was a director. He knew how to handle us. If he was disgusted by our diets or habits, he never let it show. Lovely man. Well, there was that drug-fuelled murder, but apart from that…'

Like much of Berlin, the airport was undergoing sizable reconstruction, which meant that given our mutual struggle with the German language it took a while to find where to meet Krond's friends off their flights. I never quite knew how to deal with recognising Krond's otherworldly co-stars. You could go by their appearance in posters from their heyday, but decades had passed, and who knew how they might age, if at all?

The Wolfman From Sirius seemed completely unchanged from his glory days, while The Creature From The Black Lagoon had turned grey. Krond bounded over to them, his clawed arms more than lengthy enough to surround them both. The Creature twitchily fished out a cigarette, 'We can s-s-moke in this airport, c-can't we kid?' he asked me, lighting up before I could answer. The Wolfman gave nothing away, his eyes hidden behind expensive sunglasses.

'My friends, so good to see you!' Krond's single giant unblinking eye seemed to have lit up. 'It's been far too long. Wine?'

'N-not for me, not any more – but I'll h-happily have orange juice,' began the Creature.

At the wine bar, Krond's ebullience showed no sign of abating, helped no end when an old couple sitting nearby asked for his autograph, and he was able to furnish them with a full-size signed poster. 'Say, is this it?' the Wolfman drawled as Krond wallowed in the attention, 'Just the three of us?' His barely concealed sneer revealed perfectly whitened teeth, and he began to occupy himself with his suit sleeves, making sure they were rolled up to show off his coiffured arm-hair.

I gave an update on what I knew. Qurk The Robot From Mars had recently had a bout of unsuccessful upgrade surgery, and was in seclusion until all the magnetic tape could be retightened. While The Vampire Princess Of Venus was going through her seventh acrimonious divorce and 'Vanted to be alone'. And as for The Blob …

'We didn't invite The Blob!' bellowed Krond.

'Th-th-thank goodness, the bitch! What a diva!'

*

The arrangements for the evening were going to involve The Wolfman crashing at mine, while The Creature stayed with Krond. In the end though, it didn't take much to get the three of them watching the old films again. Krond's VHS collection was immaculately kept, all the great B-movies that had featured genuine monsters taped from early Eighties TV reruns. During *10,000 Martian Maniacs*, Krond eagerly pointed out where the mirrors had been placed to make him look like an invading army. A detailed description of his humanoid co-stars' failings accompanied *The Wild Wolf-Man's Arkansas Rodeo Rampage*, while The Creature moaned that the Glorious Technicolor of *Black Lagoon Blood Fest* was less than Glorious. All three were always ready with their humorous anecdotes, mostly prepared for the next day – although the biggest whoops of derisory laughter were saved for the decade-old adverts during the commercial breaks.

We started early the next day to prepare for the convention, loading a van with the memorabilia that they all hoped to shift over the course of the long day ahead. Then the phone rang. I could tell from the moment I heard my boss's thick German accent it was work. 'Look, ja – so zer is an emergency here – you must come in.'

'Sorry, I can't come in. I've had today booked off for a long time.'

'Thomas,' he barked, making full use of the German accent's innate ability to snap angrily, 'You must to work come, it is only by working hard at your desk that you vill get any better vis your German.'

'My German is fine.'

'You think so, yes? You think you impress us vis the vay you pronounce things? You spend too much time vis zat ridiculous creature, it is always about you two. Or 'you Zwo' as you vould say.'

I recognised the derision in his last remark – an ongoing snide dig my co-workers had adopted at my attempts to use colloquial German – and put the phone down immediately. I couldn't face this argument, and there was no way I was going to disappoint Krond.

'Work again, Thomas?' Krond's head was too large to ever really peer round a door but he did the closest approximation that he was capable of. 'Forget it,' I shrugged. 'It's going to be a long day and I need to get driving.'

Berlin's first ever science fiction convention was poorly organised and overly attended. Queues became crowds became agitated mobs. We'd been allocated a relatively modest corner of the main hall within which to put our stand, and I was worried that Krond might take offence. But none of the trio I'd driven to the event were that comfortable being surrounded by too many people so it seemed to work. A steady stream of B-movie aficionados kept us busy, and the Deutschmarks flowing, and I had to run back to the van several times to stock up on merchandise.

It amazed me how much Krond enjoyed it. The same questions kept turning up, and he'd answer every time with the same level of enthusiasm, as if he'd never been asked it before. 'No you are right,' I'd hear him say repeatedly, 'Krond isn't my real name, my race don't really have names – no, it's not my stage name. It's my Monster name. My first agent in Hollywood, a wonderful man told me all about 'A monster name'. It has to be short, one or two syllables. Punchy, yet alien. That one day will be synonymous with a monster.' And even those who'd heard all the answers before at earlier conventions would laugh and enjoy the stories of a bygone Hollywood era.

This was how things should be. Not stuck in an office.

Spending ages getting people's computers to work and then having them leave English/German dictionaries lying on my desk. Dictionaries open at the words I might have once misused. And certainly not having to suffer an 'office nickname' based on my earnest attempts to speak German.

Occasionally a minor actor from the new Star Trek show would appear on the main stage, and we'd enjoy a quiet period. The Creature would make up for lost time by shoving a cigarette in each gill and power-smoking. The Wolfman would be continuing a one-on-one conversation with one of the younger female autograph hunters. Krond, however, would stay seated at the stand, just in case. This was his day, and he wasn't going to miss anyone who wanted to tell him how brilliant he'd been in 'that film where the UFO lands in a remote part of California but no-one initially believes the kids who see it'. And just before it ended, we all trooped over to a makeshift cinema to watch a rare 3D screening of Krond's finest hour, *Venusian Voodoo Vixens Versus The FBI*. Even if Krond spent most of it struggling to get some sort of extra-dimensional effect from his single, staring eye.

Finally, it was all over. We re-loaded what was left into the van, and drove The Creature to the airport for a late-night flight. We weren't quite sure where The Wolfman had got to, although reports in the Berlin press a week later did dwell on a curious decline in the city's cat population. Then at last, I parked outside Krond's building.

'Thanking you Thomas,' Krond began, 'promise, Thomas. You are a man of your word and you keep your promise.'

I smiled.

'And now, it is time for me to keep my promise. My part of the bargain. You help me with a favour, and I do one for you.'

I took a small tatty piece of paper out of my jacket pocket and placed it on the dashboard. Krond picked it up, deftly unfolded it and tried to make sense of the angry jottings, the numerous crossings out and re-writings.

'Is *everyone* you work with on this list?' Krond asked.

I nodded.

'And it is definitely disintegration you want?'

I smiled again.

Krond's eye blinked and then he laughed.

'Monstrous, Zwo, Monstrous.'

The Elephant in the Tower
David McGrath

Aaaah! J'adore l'odeur of Poissy in the morning, this little place on the outskirts of Paris, the birthplace of kings, the birthplace of my king, Louis IX, my master, mon amour, ma raison. Poissy exudes royalty, its perfectly pleached hedges, its aroma of oils and spice, tabac et parfum, its fine Dukes and Counts in tailored silks, debating philosophie and art on the lawns in the surrounds of soft harp. Even Poissy's sunshine is somehow regal, its air noble, its water majestic – oh, bon matin garçons, où est mon petit dejeuner? Attendez – wait – arretez, stop – get your hands off of me – where are we going? Louis! Louis! They are taking me! Unhand me, sir! Louis!

Day 1

I have been kidnapped by the English, whipped and smacked inside a box then carted to Hell, a stinking, rainy, festering, muddy-muck, flea-ridden, soiled, bubonic hideousness of a Hell.

I have yet to be told of a reason.

I have yet to be officially received by nobility.

I have been simply kidnapped, stolen across the sea and locked in the Tower. There are three lions already imprisoned here and when I called to them for some sort of explanation, they roared me quiet because I had woken them. A mangy polar bear then sauntered over and asked my name without a third party's introduction, just *alright there, geezer! What's your name then?* I don't know what came over me but I was not going to stand there and be asked my name without knowing the asker's title or standing. I, well, it's indecent but I ran at him. Shackles were placed upon my feet as result, these jailors declaring me unruly. The cretins! There is such a disgusting smell in this place. They have constructed a box for me to sleep in, no bigger than half of me. Tomorrow I shall wake up in Poissy, in Louis's arms, and this will all have been a foul nightmare.

Day 2
The lions tell me I am in London, and to keep calm. London's people stare. They are desperate for staring. They arrived from all around the city to stare. I woke to staring. The Beast they call me. The beast! The beast is about ten years old, one Beefeater keeps telling them, possessing a rough hide rather than fur, has small eyes at the top of its head, and eats and drinks with a trunk. As though nobody in this insidious, stinking hole has ever seen an elephant before, swarming around at all sides of me with toothless grins, laughing and making faces. I shouted *Louis will have your heads* but they just kept laughing.

Then, the polar bear appeared from the river with a fish in his mouth, shit dripping from it, and they all cheer!

'I apologise for my behaviour, yesterday,' I said.

Then he said, he said – 'Don't worry old chap, water off me hairy ball-sack.'

What sort of place is this where such language is used?

Then there is a zebra, a drunken slut of an animal, who drinks beer with the Beefeaters in their canteen.

'Hello, handsome,' she says. 'You're a big boy. They say once you go elephant! What sort of equipment you got down there, love?' Then she inspects my...

'That's some set of crown jewels alright,' she says and trots off, the ghastly thing.

Tonight I long for Louis. I see him in his finest armour, storming the Tower with a battalion of men and burning it to the ground, freeing me as we freed him in Egypt, then we return to Poissy where he bathes me clean with coconut milk.

Day 3

I wish for death.

King Henry III arrived and I said, finally, this mess, this bloody mess will be rectified.

'Your Majesty,' I said. 'This has obviously been some dreadful mistake. I belong to King Louis IX of France. I live in Poissy.'

'Who is it from?' he said.

'It is a gift from King Louis IX of France, your Majesty,' said a Beefeater.

And my heart burst an ocean of pain into my chest. Louis, *my master, mon amour, ma raison* had given me away like a sack of potatoes. There are no words.

'Looks a bit like old Louis,' said King Henry and everyone laughed. The sycophants. 'What's the beast's name?'

'We were waiting for you to name it, your Majesty.'

'Let's call him – Simpleton. What does he eat?'

'We were hoping you would know, your Majesty.'

'Of course I know,' he shouted. 'It's an elephant. It eats – beef and red wine. Now feed it. The poor beast looks starved.'

And with that, he left, and there are no words, and they placed a piece of cow in front of me for supper and a barrel of red wine, and there are no words, and I wish for death.

Day 13

I was starved and malnourished and had gone two weeks without eating. There is nothing here, no music, no insight. The monkeys throw shit and sometimes the patterns are interesting but there is nobody to converse about the deeper meaning. Death was just about here and I welcomed it. All of a sudden, the Beefeaters held me at the neck and forced a slab of beef down my throat then poured the barrel of red wine down my gullet. I am truly forsaken.

Day 26

They burn women upon Tower Hill. It is the reason for the stench. The accused stand in front of three or four cardinals with a barbarian crowd booing and cheering behind them. The accused perform their defence. More often than not, they are found guilty by the cardinals and burnt alive, much to the delight of the masses. I hate this place.

I am regularly eating beef and drinking red wine. They will not give me anything else! I long for water, for fresh vegetables, for crunchy hay, for fruit and nutrition, for decent cuisine.

Day 43

Today there may be some hope. An ostrich was presented to King Henry by the King of Belgium. The ostrich is of nobility and hates this place, too. They throw her nails and metal to eat because somehow, the King thinks ostriches eat metal. He concocts these stories when he is under pressure, and then, after repeating the story several times, he genuinely believes them as the truth.

'Escape,' the ostrich whispered to me tonight. 'I know a way.'

The snitching zebra then came into earshot and we hushed. But it was enough to dream with – escape. The ostrich has given me hope. I will not go back to France. We will go south, catch passage to Africa where we can live free with the wild animals there on the plains. And life will once again be sweet. The ostrich indeed, has given me hope.

Day 45

The ostrich died yesterday. The menagerie's vet said it was a witch's curse and not as result of the twenty three nails she had eaten. Seven years in medical school and all the man can say is witch's curse. Perhaps that was the escape she spoke of. The Beefeaters picked a woman out of the crowd and burnt her alive for casting a curse on the royal ostrich. I have to say here in private, I enjoyed it. My grief had somewhere to go – even if it was at the end of a pointed finger without reason. I had goosebumps and in the excitement, drank my whole barrel of red wine.

'Thirsty today, Simpleton?' said a Beefeater, and rolled me over a second barrel. I drank that, too and found myself roaring along with the mob.

'Burn her!' I shouted. 'Burn the witch!'

I woke today sore and ashamed, with an ache in my head and back. No more red wine, I said, trying to stand, only to find a group of leery builders on my back with brick and mortar, talking of big-titted conquests whilst building a structure. Apparently King Henry read in a book that elephants could support enough weight on their backs for a castle. I drank red wine to take the edge off.

Day 143

Waaahey! Simpleton the elephant. The Tower! Fuck my balls. My big elephant balls. Me and the monkeys flung shit at the lions. Haha! Those fuckin' lions. Think they're so great. Fuck 'em. No, haha! I'm goin' now to fuck that zebra bitch. Where is she?

Day 236

The hangovers. I am voiceless in my hangovers, deadened and null. I can barely find time between them to write. I find myself wailing for more wine as soon as I wake just to quell them. My behaviour over the last few months has been disgraceful. The zebra and I have done some atrocious things. I have fallen out with the lions and the polar bear. The new leopard has been told to stay well away from me. The only things I look forward to now are the witch burnings. One is on tonight at eight o' clock. 'Burn the witch,' I will shout. 'Burn her!'

I cannot even remember what I'm angry about? I just know I'm angry. They say an elephant never forgets but I cannot retain any longer, I cannot – retain.

Afterwards, we will souse ourselves on ale and wine. And the Beefeaters will lock the doors and we will break and damage and roar, pot-valiant and brave, and we will talk of escape and rebellion because we are the ones with the strength. They only have the keys and funny hats. And then we will sleep and start it over.

I never needed God in Poissy. But this place, this place has made a believer out of me, because if there is a Hell, this is it, and if there is a Hell, there must be a Heaven, there must be.

I need wine.

Day 435
We took Egypt together, Louis! Do you remember? And I stood by you when you were captured. A whole two years. Do you remember, Louis? We took Egypt, Louis. *Joyeux Noel*. I hope you are happy.

Day 500
500th day in the Tower. More wine! More wine, Beefeaters! They don't know. They don't even know, the fools. You are fools! They don't know me! You've all come to see the elephant? Well, here I am! Are you not entertained? Step right up and see Simpleton the elephant! More wine!

Day 579

Last night I found myself dumbfounded on a sea of elephants, a lost elephant. Simpleton the elephant, floating atop a sea of elephants, a million elephants deep and a million elephants wide, a raging sea of elephants, and I couldn't ascertain which elephant was me. I tried hard to find myself, but every elephant looked the same, and I could have been any one of them, and we just raged hard in the squall, giant waves, a thousand elephants high, crashing and turning and swirling…

Day 622

The ravens have gathered, squawking dinner, and methinks they will have it soon. I am a dying thing, diary. The menagerie's vet inspected me today.

They are burning the witch now.

If I could save the poor woman, I would.

It is the Kings who shuffle us like this, I'd tell them, it is the Queens who point out our villain, but my words, if I could speak them, would do her no good. These people do not want truth, because if the truth were to be heard, their grand illusion would crumble, as has mine.

So here I'll lie until the end, in my little box behind the great big wall, watching witch-hunts as the Kings and Queens go unobserved in their devilment, and I'll drink your cheap wine and eat the stewed and toxic meat you serve. I will breathe your smoke and I will carry your stone on my back and pray at night for better days. I'll be your pickled savage, your placid simpleton and you will hear no more a peep from me.

You have come to see the elephant?

You have seen him.

ABOUT THE AUTHORS

Alan Graham studied 'Creative Writing' and 'Economics' at UEA and is still unsure which discipline relies on make-believe the most.

Alex Smith lives in Cape Town with her partner, their book-eating baby boy and their dogs. She has had four novels published in South Africa (Random House/Umuzi Imprint), was shortlisted for the 2010 Caine Prize and won the 2011 Nielsens Bookseller's Choice Award.

Andrew Lloyd-Jones was born in London, and grew up in Alaska. He won the Fish Prize with his story 'Feathers and Cigarettes', and his writing has featured in the Tales of the Decongested anthologies, in the Canongate collection *Original Sins* and in the Pulp.net anthology *Down the Angel*. He is currently Short Fiction Editor for Litro Magazine, and host of Liars' League NYC.

Angela Trevithick travels far and wide where she can. She spends the bulk of her time dreaming about battles at sea and piratical greed as she works on novels for young readers, and is fortunate to have published short stories in between. Notable publications include Emerge: New Australian Writing, Vibewire and Sherbert Magazine.

Barry McKinley's play, *Elysium Nevada,* was nominated for Best New Play, Irish Theatre Awards 2010. He has been short-listed on two occasions for the Hennessy Literary Award and has written plays for BBC Radio 4 and RTE.

C. T. Kingston is a slow but steady writer, having been published in various flash fiction magazines over the last few years, as well as having had stories performed by actors at the Liars' League in London and Leeds. She is currently writing a play.

Christopher Samuels is a pseudonym ...

David McGrath studied Creative & Life Writing at Goldsmiths University. His first novel, *Rickshaw* follows Irish, a rickshaw rider, around the West End. Once upon a time, he gave walking tours of London to sulky teenagers. The story about the elephant in the tower saved him on numerous occasions.

David Malone's other short stories have appeared in Carve Magazine, Momaya Annual Review, Grey Sparrow Journal, and Crannog Literary Magazine. *The Love Below* was long-listed for the Fish International Short Story Prize.

David Mildon is an actor and playwright who pays the gas bill by telling tourists the story of London. However, the woman he loves prefers listening to tall tales, so sometimes he writes them down.

Raised in a tiny Alaskan fishing village, educated at Yale University, **Derek Ivan Webster** appreciates a good contrast. The freelance lifestyle would have long ago driven him mad if not for the balm of his sage wife and their four precious/precocious little conspirators.

Ellen O'Neill created stories and poems from kindergarten to the present. She wrote two short stories published in the Chrysalis Reader and writes feature stories in local and international newspapers, and also writes song lyrics – she even writes resumés for job seekers.

James Smyth was born in a small town in West Yorkshire, and moved to London to seek fame and fortune as a writer. The fortune hasn't arrived at the time of writing, but the fame must surely be just around the corner.

Jonathan Pinnock has had stuff published all over the place, including the BBC. His novel *Mrs Darcy versus the Aliens* was published by Proxima in September 2011 and was followed in 2012 by his Salt short story collection *Dot Dash*.

Joshan Esfandiari Martin is a writer and film director living in Berlin.

Lee Reynoldson learnt his craft in Bootcamp Keegan, a hardworking online writers' community. He now writes fantasy adventure stories for fun and occasionally profit.

Lennart Lundh is a short-fiction writer, poet, historian, and photographer. His work has appeared internationally, in some forty journals and anthologies, since 1965.

Maria Kyle is a freelance magazine editor. In between jobs, she is working on building a collection of short stories.

To everyone's great relief, **Nichol Wilmor** did not follow in his parents' footsteps and join the theatrical profession. Instead he became a random traveller, an unreliable teacher and an accidental publisher. He now writes – very slowly – under different names.

Peng Shepherd's fiction has appeared in Litro, .Cent Magazine, and Liars' League, among others. She is currently an MFA Stein Fellow in Creative Writing at New York University, where she also teaches as an adjunct undergraduate instructor. She is finishing her first novel.

Rebecca J Payne is a science fiction author. She has previously had work published in Interzone, Ethereal Tales and Dark Currents.

Recently returned from a stint in New York, **Richard Meredith** is readjusting slowly to life in the UK. He studied English at York University and has spent the last ten years working in television. He has published more nonfiction and journalism than fiction so far, and is working on changing that.

Richard Smyth is a freelance writer. He has published two non-fiction books: *Bumfodder* (Souvenir Press, 2012) and *Bloody British History: Leeds* (The History Press, 2013) and has had short fiction published in The Stinging Fly, The Fiction Desk, .Cent, Vintage Script and a Spilling Ink anthology.

Tom McKay is a lecturer and writer. He currently lives in Paris above a bar. Despite this he is still trying to write a novel.

The Editors

Katy Darby co-runs Liars' League. She teaches short story and novel writing at City University, London. Her first novel *The Unpierced Heart*, aka *The Whores' Asylum* is published by Penguin.

Cherry Potts is the author of two collections of short stories: *Mosaic of Air,* and *Tales Told Before Cockcrow*; and a photographic diary *The Blackheath Onegin*. She has had several stories in anthologies. She runs workshops for writers exploring NLP approaches to language and characterisation.